Marshmallow Magic and the Wild Rose Rouge

Also by Karen McCombie:

The *Ally's World* series
A Guided Tour of Ally's World
My V. Groovy Ally's World Journal
The *Stella Etc.* series

To find out more about Karen McCombie,
visit her website
www.karenmccombie.com

Marshmallow Magic and the Wild Rose Rouge

KAREN McCOMBIE

SCHOLASTIC
PRESS

Scholastic Children's Books,
Commonwealth House, 1-19 New Oxford Street,
London, WC1A 1NU, UK
a division of Scholastic Ltd
London ~ New York ~ Toronto ~ Sydney ~ Auckland
Mexico City ~ New Delhi ~ Hong Kong

First published in the UK by Scholastic Ltd, 2004
This edition published by Scholastic Ltd, 2005

ISBN 0 439 95956 X

Printed and bound by Nørhaven Paperback A/S, Denmark

2 4 6 8 10 9 7 5 3 1

For Stanley, who was there,
and then wasn't

☆ CONTENTS ☆

1

Shhh. . .

Hello.

My name's Lemmie.

Do you want to know a secret?

The secret is, I've got *lots* of secrets.

Some of my secrets are so old I've kind of half-forgotten them.

Some are around me all the time, every day.

Some are so weird I can't tell anyone about them, 'cause they'd laugh at me or think I was a freak. (Well, drawing circles around the freckles on your arms when you're sleepwalking *is* pretty freaky, I guess.)

Some of my secrets are so spangly and special that I hold them inside of me, like a sparkler in the dark.

My secrets come in all shapes and sizes: some are

weeny and floaty-light; some are heart-shaped, and some are, er . . . mouse-shaped.

One secret in particular's so *humungously* big, I can't even bring myself to think about it, never mind write it down. . .

But then some of my secrets can be amazingly, dazzlingly *ordinary* too. Like with Dad, I could *never* tell him that his hip Liam Gallagher haircut looks less hip and more like a deranged farmer's attacked him with a pair of sheep shears. That chunklet of truth would be *way* too cruel.

And with Mum, I can't exactly let her know that the "cute" knock-knock thing we do when she comes to my bedroom door is just something I invented to give me time to hide any stray marshmallow magic under the bed.

Speaking of Mum and Dad, they know a couple of my secrets, but not all of them.

My best friends Morven and Jade, they know some of the marshmallow magic, but that's about it.

There's only one person who knows everything about *everything*, and that's Rose Rouge (of course).

Oh, and before I forget, here's another secret: Lemmie's not my real name.

Confused yet?

Hey, welcome to the club – I manage to confuse myself *all* the time. . .

2

A feather a day

"Knock-knock!" Mum shouts from the other side of the door, at the same time as she knock-knocks for real.

"Who's there?" I ask, hurriedly slapping the lid of the shoebox back on and shoving it under my bed.

(Urgh . . . now the feathers are sticking to my hand. I shouldn't have started looking through them after I'd scooped peanut butter straight from the jar with my finger.)

"Harry!" Mum calls out.

"Harry who?" I call back, jumping up and trying to wipe my fluffy, peanut-butter-covered fingers on my jeans. (What a klutz.)

"Harry up and open the door!" says Mum.

Yeah, yeah, it's a really corny joke – just like every

other knock-knock joke we know – but it's a nice way to get a bit of privacy, and not have my parents barge in on me without being asked.

Anyway, I go to turn the door knob with my left hand as usual, and then realize I'm going to end up covering *it* with feathery fluff and peanut butter too, so I shove my hand behind my back instead, out of sight. Out of *Mum*'s sight, I mean. Who needs awkward questions, like "What's with the feathers?" and "Why does a daughter of mine have to be so weird?"

"Hey, Laurel!" Mum smiles, standing on the tiny landing at the top of the tiny set of stairs to my tiny room.

(Hands up if you've just spotted my real name, by the way.)

Ah, there goes Mum; doing her customary blink for a second or two. Coming up from downstairs, my room's always a bit of a shock to her senses, I reckon. Downstairs is all low-lights and off-whites and soft-suede and clutter-free calm, like an interior designer's show-home (which it *is*, since my parents are both interior designers). Upstairs is . . . the opposite.

It's so small up here in the attic that there's more low, sloping ceiling than there is wall-space, but that just makes it easier to decorate. The trouble is, I just don't think Mum and Dad totally *get* the flurry of butterflies (cut out from sheets of wrapping paper and Blu-tacked all over the walls), *or* the chilli-pepper fairy lights, *or* the fact that I painted each chunk of wall and ceiling a different colour. I guess they think I just sort of *whammed* it all together, but I didn't. I always give *everything* a lot of thought, even if it doesn't seem that way to anyone who happens to be watching. It's like with the paint; I didn't just pick the colours for their colour (if you see what I mean) – I picked them for their names too: "Rainbird Green", "Lemon Haze", "Peacock Blue", "Gingersnap", "Sugared Lilac" and . . . and what was the name for the bright red again? I can't remember. Wasn't it something like—

"Been busy swotting, then?" says Mum, interrupting my thoughts.

She's teasing. I can tell because she's leaning casually on the doorframe – her shoulder right next to Isla (my door angel) – trying to hide a puzzled smile as she stares at my head.

Oops . . . I forgot about my hair. Before I started sifting through my shoebox of feathers, I'd been playing around with it, trying to fix it into a bun with two plastic chopsticks we got when we last went to the Chinese restaurant (run by my friend Jade's grandparents) in the town square.

I shoot my (left) hand up and pat the lopsided

bird's-nest that's landsliding its way down towards my shoulder.

"Um, I was just trying something out," I say, suddenly dropping my hand back down and turning my head to one side a little, in case Mum can spot any telltale smears of peanut-buttery fluff on my mousey-brown bird's-nest.

Befuddled: that's what Mum looks like, looking at me. I think I befuddle her quite a lot.

Freeze-frame us both right now and you might start to see why. . .

MUM: Shiny, plum-coloured hair; perfect, neat bob, cut above the chin.

ME: A mousy, fuzzy bird's-nest, decorated with chopsticks, feathers and peanut-butter grease.

MUM: Navy T-shirt, pressed jeans, navy loafers.

ME: Tie-dye vest top, daisy-covered pyjama bottoms, one blue flip-flop, one pink flip-flop.

MUM: A dainty pair of sapphire blue stud earrings, her white-gold wedding ring.

ME: A Luckenbooth necklace (present from Rose Rouge), a dragonfly tattoo on my shoulder and a Hello Kitty tattoo on my hip (free along with a load of other temporary tattoos with the last copy of *Bliss* magazine).

Spot the difference.

Y'know, sometimes when she opens the door of

my room Mum stares at me and I think she's wondering who this stranger is in the family. (Still, at least I'm just *weird*, and not wild, like Rose Rouge, and not as much of a stranger either, when it comes down to it. . .)

"Listen, Laurel," says Mum, reaching over and swiping a straggle of hair away from my face, "*Mrs Doubtfire*'s just started on TV – do you want to come down and watch it with me and Dad?"

"Nah, I better revise for this French test tomorrow."

I'd *definitely* better – I've done nothing but muck around and daydream since I came up here to my room after tea.

Mum looks a bit disappointed, but then I know her and Dad would much rather watch some dreary documentary on BBC4 about the history of concrete in modern design or whatever.

"Well, let me at least take that stuff down to the kitchen, out of your way," says Mum, spotting the tray on my ratty old patterned Persian carpet. I catch her frowning slightly at the sight of the opened jar of peanut butter, the two glasses (one of half-drunk orange juice, one of half-drunk lemonade), the plate from last night's cheese toastie and the sticky Maltesers bag.

Mess of any kind gives Mum the heebie-jeebies.

Which means she stays out of my room a lot, which is perfect. (I love my parents, and I love my room – they just don't mix.)

With a wave, and a clunk of the door, Mum's gone, leaving me in my muddled oasis again.

And speaking of muddles, maybe I need to explain stuff; stuff like Isla (my door angel), and the marshmallow magic, and Rose Rouge. But maybe I'll just start with where I live . . . oh, and the feathers, since I can do that at the same time. (Don't worry, it'll get less muddled. I think. I *hope*.)

So where do I start?

Three-hundred-and-eleven days ago, that's where, 'cause that's how long we've lived here in Balgownie. (Me, Mum, Dad, but *not* Rose Rouge.)

I know for a fact that it's three-hundred-and-eleven days, because I've picked up a feather and kept it for every single day we've been here.

So here's the thing about the feather thing: we used to live in Edinburgh, which is the capital city of Scotland and is very cool, with great old buildings and a castle towering over the shops in the High Street. As far as big cities go, it's not *London* huge, but it's still *pretty* huge, with streets and roads and pavements criss-crossing and overlapping for ever and ever amen.

And then we moved to Balgownie, which is a

small town, kind of not quite in the Highlands, and the pavements lead to the country, and the streets and the roads amble to the river on one side and a great big wooded hill on the other. Driving into the town on that first day three-hundred-and-eleven days ago, I saw silvery fish jumping in the river and a spindly-legged deer stopped *just* long enough in the middle of the road to give us all heart attacks before it bounded over a fence and into the forest.

That first day, while Mum and Dad tried to get the lock on the front door of our new house to work, a feather fluttered and floated down out of the cloud-speckled sky and landed *splat* at my feet. I kicked at it with the toe of my trainer at first, like I was scared it was full of toxic country germs, or that it would flutter back up and tickle my knees or something.

"It's a lucky sign, you doughball!" I heard Rose Rouge say, even though she was far, far away, back in Edinburgh.

A lucky sign; I knew I could do with one of those, since the past three years had been pretty much lucky with a capital "U" and "N" slapped right before it.

So without mentioning anything to my parents (who were too busy squabbling over keys to worry about lucky signs fluttering from the sky), I picked the feather up, shoved it in my pocket, and decided to keep it in my room.

And *then* I decided that a girl can never have too many lucky signs and I've looked for a feather every day since. I've kept my feather collection secret from Mum and Dad because they'd just think it was deeply weird, and try and give me one of their gentle "you can't go believing in superstition" talks. And I guess picking up a feather every day *is* kind of weird, if you see the world in a straightforward way (like my parents), instead of from a pleasantly squint angle (like me).

So that's the story of the feathers and my room un-muddled (hopefully). Now to explain about Isla, and the marshmallow magic, and Rose Rouge (my best friend, my hero, my big sis).

But there's no time right now, 'cause of revising for this stupid French test tomorrow. The way things are going, I'll need a miracle (or some marshmallow magic) just to pass. . .

3

Magic, only marshmallow-flavoured

It's 8.58 a.m., and B.T.F.T. (before the French test).

Me and my two best friends are sitting on the wall outside school, staring up at Craigandarroch hill and wishing we were right at the top, counting clouds, instead of waiting for the school bell of doom.

"Crisp?" offers Morven.

"Thanks," I say, dipping my hand into her half-finished bag of Quavers.

"Crisp?"

"Yuck – no thanks," says Jade. "You *know* the smell of them always reminds me of old trainers."

Morven doesn't respond, she's too busy melting in front of our very eyes.

"Wow, I'm *boiling*," she moans, unsticking a long tendril of fair hair from her damp face and tucking it behind her ear. "Wish I was up on the hill, where at least there's a breeze!"

Morven McGregor is tall, skinny and overheats easily. I think that's because she comes from generations of farmers who've been used to mucking out cattle and shepherding sheep in the depths of icy Scottish winters, with only a cosy jersey and a cheery whistle to keep frostbite at bay. For a girl who calls gale-force winds "fresh" and thinks gloves are for wimps – even when you're making snowballs – the hint of end-of-May summery-ness seems to have brought Morven out in a heat rash.

"It's *not* boiling, Morv!" says Jade, shading her dark, almond eyes from the sun with her hand as she gazes around at our friend. "You should have been on holiday with us in Gran Canaria last year – the tar on the road was *melting* it was so hot!"

Jade Song is small, pretty and porcelain doll-ish, as if she's never sweated a day in her life, never mind mucked out a cow or shepherded a sheep. Like me, she's a city girl (from Glasgow), though she's been a Balgownie local for a year longer than I have. She's very popular, mainly because shortly after her and her mum and dad moved here, her grandparents arrived too and opened the town's favourite restaurant, The Jade Palace – which was *way* more exciting and exotic than the shortbread'n'scone café on the High Street or the fish'n'chip shop on Dee Street.

Actually, Morven's pretty popular too, because a) she's easy-going and fun, and b) her farm on the edge of town is a bit of an open house; anyone passing is more than welcome to wander in and pat a lamb or eat one of the stodgy cakes Morv's mum is forever baking.

And I guess I'm sort of popular too, even if it's just 'cause of being Morven and Jade's (on-the-verge-of-kooky) mate. But being popular, even just a little bit popular-*ish*, it's a funny feeling for me, considering I was treated like a leper with bad breath at my last school, all because of—

"Er, what's with the stone, Lemmie?" asks Morven, glancing down at the small circular hunk of rock I'm rolling around in the palm of my hand.

"It's not a stone, it's a fossil," says Jade, matter-of-factly.

Jade says everything matter-of-factly, even jokes. Which makes her not very good at telling jokes, actually.

"OK, so it's a *fossil*," says Morven. "So why've you got it, Lemmie?"

"It's going to help me pass the French test."

Morven looks confused, and stares harder at the stone, as if she's looking for a very tiny list of French words scribbled on it.

"Um . . . what's a fossil got to do with passing the French test, Lem?"

"It's to help me concentrate."

"Is this one of your marshmallow magic things, then?" asks Morven, scrunching around in her crisp bag for the last Quaver or three.

"Uh-huh. Rose Rouge found it on a beach once and gave it to me. She said she looked it up and it was an ancient type of mini squid called an ammonite, and it's at *least* seventy million years old."

"An ammonite," Jade repeats, filing that bit of info into her computer of a mind. (She's very smart; she'll pass the French test no problem, with no need for any kind of magic, marshmallow-flavoured or not.)

"Seventy *million* years old? What – *that* bit of stone?!"

Morven nearly chokes on a Quaver in surprise.

"Yep. Rose Rouge said that if my brain was ever in a tangle over whatever, this fossil would be perfect to focus on. 'Cause something that's seventy million years old makes you realize that a twenty-minute French test isn't *anything* to stress about at *all*."

"So . . . so you mean it's like *really* wise, and it'll

give you the answers to the test?" asks Morven, missing the point completely and going off at a tangent.

Then *blam!*, the bell goes bling, and everyone around spins into this big, loud hubbub, so it's not really the time to explain to Morven that no, some old fossil can't exactly whisper the English translation for "*singe*" to me in class. Marshmallow magic doesn't work like that.

Marshmallow magic works like *this*. . .

Right, for a start, forget about witches and Gandalf and Harry Potter and that lot. And don't go thinking that my sister showed me how to make milk-floats levitate or squirrels turn into unicorns or members of famous boy bands fall instantly in love with me or anything.

The magic Rose Rouge taught me was soft and pink and sweet, "like Turkish Delight, or marshmallows!" she said, when she first let me in on the Rainbow Breathing. That happened this one time back in Edinburgh, when I came home from school feeling terrible about something or other (there were always plenty of something-or-others going on then), and Rose Rouge did her best to try and help me feel a bit less terrible.

I didn't get what Rose was saying at first (I was too busy hiccuping between crying), but when I did the Rainbow Breathing with her, I *felt* the magic working.

"Close your eyes and picture a red flower opening slowly," she told me. "And now *breathe*, just as slowly. OK, do the same with a yellow one. . ."

[*Breathe*]

". . .and pink. . ."

[*Breathe*]

". . .and green. . ."

[*Breathe*]

By the time I'd got through orange and purple and blue, I'd stopped crying, I'd stopped hiccuping, I was breathing slower, feeling calmer.

And after that, Rose taught me loads more marshmallow magic, like Roll of the Dice (great for figuring out what kind of day you've got in store), Star-Singing (good for when you're about to do something scary) and Tree-Touching (brilliant for when you're in need of a bit of protection).

"It's like we're in a secret club now!" Rose said to me, all out-of-breath from the Angry Dancing (draw the face of someone who's upsetting you on a big piece of paper, put your favourite LOUDEST, *FASTEST* track on the CD, and dance all over them).

"Yeah!" I laughed, feeling dizzy and daft and delirious.

"So we need special names for our secret club!"

she grinned at me, her long, dark dreadlocks swivelling out as she twirled, the tiny bells braided into them tinkling. "I'll be . . . Rose . . . Rose *Rouge*! And *you* could be Laurel. . ."

The newly named Rose Rouge glanced around my pink and red bedroom (just the two colours of paint on the walls of my old room, unlike the six in my room here). She stopped when she saw the half-empty plastic bottle of lemonade sticking out of my school-bag.

". . .Laurel Lemon!"

I loved it.

I know it sounds like a kid's name, but I *was* only a kid at the time (I was nine then, I'm nearly thirteen now). And I *love*d that Rose Rouge nicknamed me "Lemmie" after a while, even if my parents didn't like it at all and refused to call me anything but Laurel. Even now, I know Mum and Dad hate that I asked everyone to call me Lemmie when I started at Balgownie Academy, including the teachers.

By the way, if you don't happen to live in Scotland then you won't know that the first year of secondary school here is called (drum roll, please) First Year. And I started in First Year just a few days after we moved to Balgownie.

"First Year: it's like the first year of a whole new *everything*!" said Rose Rouge, when I spoke to her the night before I met my classmates and my soon-to-be best friends, Morven and Jade.

Rose Rouge was right (of *course* she was; isn't she always?).

That's the amazing thing about starting somewhere new; you can be whoever you want to be. If you've always had bunches in your hair, you can turn up on Day One with a mohican, and everyone'll think that's what you've always looked like.

Or if you're bored of being shy, you can try to be braver, and no one *ever* needs to know that you used to be so nervy that just standing up in class and reading something aloud used to make you feel like *barfing* all over your school-desk.

You could be some freak (like me) who hadn't had what you could call a proper friend in three years, and end up with the best mates in the world (Morven and Jade, who smiled and pointed to an empty seat beside them on my very first day).

Yep, I loved being in First Year. The different friends, the different name, the different *me* . . . it all fitted together, a whole new brilliant beginning, just like Rose Rouge said.

The only *non*-brilliant thing about it was Rose Rouge staying behind in Edinburgh, so she could go to art school. . .

"Lemmie! C'mon! Mrs Fraser will flip out if we're

late!" says Morven, hurrying me away from the view of Craigandarroch – not that I could see it with all my daydreaming getting in the way.

I have to go. There's a French test waiting that won't go away, and a seventy-million-year-old fossil that's going to help me not fail (hopefully)...

It's 11.01 a.m., and A.T.F.T. (after the French test).

It's also breaktime and I have absolutely *no* idea how I got on in the French test. All I do know is that I don't feel too freaked out, unlike Morven, who is *so* convinced she's bombed it badly that she can hardly eat her second packet of Quavers of the day.

"What do you call a meerkat with an elephant on its head?" Jade asks Morven, very seriously.

Uh-oh. This sounds like a joke, meant to cheer Morven up. But the way Jade tells jokes, it sounds about as funny as scoring minus twelvety in your French vocabulary test.

"Squashed?" I suggest, flipping myself upside-down on to my hands and slapping my mismatching flip-flops against the grey granite stones of the school wall.

"Yep. Have you heard that one before?" asks Jade, who's now a wrong-way-round small Chinese person from this angle.

"Mmmm. . ." I nod, wondering what an upside-down nod looks like.

"Wish *I* could do handstands."

That's Morven, slinking down the wall on to her haunches, so her head's a little bit closer to mine. She starts feeding me her Quavers. It feels quite interestingly weird to eat this way up. (This way *down*?)

"Y'know, you wouldn't be able to do that in a skirt, Lemmie."

Jade, settling herself in front of me cross-legged, is frighteningly sensible and practical, as always.

She's got a point about the skirt thing, even though my baggy trousers are now sagging their way down to my thighs, so they look more like a rumpled pair of shorts or something. I did once try to do a handstand at my primary school back in Edinburgh, which was posh and private and where they made you wear these hideous yellow-and-black tartan kilts. I don't know what made me do it – I think for a second I just forgot I wasn't at home, mucking about with Rose Rouge in the garden. All of a sudden I threw myself into a handstand, and couldn't figure out why all the girls in the playground were laughing and pointing at me.

Let's just say I could never face wearing those Charlie's Angels knickers again. . .

DOINK.

That's not just the sound of the fossil clattering out of my pocket and on to the tarmac; it's the noise of my heart splatting like a chucked pancake against my ribcage.

"Oh . . . my . . . God. . ." whispers Morven, a Quaver held halfway to my mouth.

"What?" says Jade, swivelling her dark, shiny head of hair around to see what Morven can see and what I can see upside-down.

"Kyle Strachan just waved at you, Lemmie!"

I don't need Jade to tell me that; I can see it for myself. Kyle Strachan – the cutest boy in First Year at Balgownie Academy – is passing by, grinning my way, and looking almost as cute the wrong way round as he does the right way up. He's just kind of *sandy*-coloured, from his hair to his freckles to his sun-tanned skin. He's like Häagen Dazs banoffee ice cream topped with caramel syrup, and almost as yummy.

And it's completely amazing that he's just waved at me.

The mistake I make is trying to wave back.

It's pretty tricky when you're doing a handstand, let me tell you.

"Erk!!"

Kyle Strachan isn't so much smiling as laughing

now, but that's no big surprise since I've just got myself in a messy girl pile with my legs tangled around Morven's shoulders and my chin scraping along the ground. (Oh, *boy*, am I a klutz. . .)

"It's OK – he thinks you're funny," Jade whispers, disentangling a strand of Morven's dark hair from the button on the pocket of my cargo pants.

"He thinks I'm a drongo," I say, rubbing the grit out of my chin.

Kyle Strachan is not only the cutest boy in our year, he's the coolest too. His sandy hair's swept up into a fin. He's an expert on hip-hop. His last girlfriend was Helena McCloud, who does ballet-dancing, wears designer clothes and looks like a thirteen-year-old version of Posh Spice. I really would have to be a drongo to think he could ever fancy a muppet like me.

"Look, you just need to talk to him *properly* sometime, Lemmie! And mumbling 'hi!' once in a while doesn't count!"

That's easy for Morven to say (well, it's not, actually, since her head's attached to my trousers).

But how *do* you talk to a boy you like a lot? Specially after he's seen you do a snazzy handstand that turns into a cruddy body-crumble. . .

"You could make a joke of what just happened," suggests Jade, as she finally frees Morven. "Next time you're near him, you could say, 'Did you see my handstand go wrong? I'll *never* get into the University of Stuntmen now!'"

Jade, Jade, Jade . . . she's good at lots of stuff, but being funny isn't one of them.

"Yeah, Jade, I *could* say that, and he *could* think my jokes were even more lame than my handstands!"

"*I* know, Lemmie! Why don't you go up to Kyle and ask him if *his* class has had to do a French test this morning, same as ours?"

Morven's suggestion is even more lame than Jade's. I like my best mates a lot, but I think I need to use my Phone-a-Friend option over this. Or Phone-a-Sister, more like.

Rose Rouge'll know what to do . . . she'll know the right thing to say.

And Rose Rouge'll know what kind of marshmallow magic I need to make Kyle Strachan dream sweet dreams of drongo little me.

Or just a spell to make him forget he ever saw me falling over and embarrassing myself would do. . .

4

In the wilds with Rose

Here are some facts about Rose Rouge:
    She's eighteen.
    She's entirely fabulous.
    She's my idol, my hero, a star.
    She's fun (in a wild way) and wild (in a funny way).
    She's a brilliant artist.
    She dresses like she raided a fancy dress shop in the dark (yes, she's worse than me).
    She collects jewellery with hearts on.
    She smells like candyfloss and jasmine.
    She lives in a grotty student flat in Edinburgh.
    She's the best sister a girl could ever have.
    She knows how to keep a secret – specially *my* secrets – better than anyone.

She's the only one who really understood and really tried to help during that whole, horrible time back in Edinburgh when—

"'Nother one?" asks Rose Rouge.

Me and Rose, we're walking through the woods that surround the old Craigandarroch Lodge, at the foot of the hill. Other ramblers have neat nylon rucksacks filled with water bottles and cling-film-wrapped sandwiches. My sister – in her scarlet velvet dress, black leggings and Doc Marten boots hand-painted with tiny flowers – is holding out a rustly bag of marshmallows to me. Her cheeks are bulging like a hamster's after a snack attack.

"Yeah, I'll have another one, if you've left me any!" I say, dipping the pointy stick I found on the ground into the bag and spearing myself a fluffy, puffy pink splodge of sweet gloop.

"One for you, fifteen for me! That's fair, isn't it, Lemmie? After all, I *am* the older sister!"

I love (and live for) the weekends that Rose Rouge comes to visit. She could tease me for the whole of the thirty-six hours she's here if she wanted to, I wouldn't mind. Pity she seems to be coming less and less often, but I guess she's got assignments and friends and a whole new life, same as me. But when Rose *does* show up – with wrists and hair jingling with jewellery – I keep her all to myself, too greedy for the shorter and shorter spells of time we spend together to even share her with my best friends.

"But *I'm* the youngest, so aren't you meant to look after *me*? Aren't you meant to spoil me rotten?" I tease back, watching my feet as I walk so no stray tree-roots trip me up. (I don't need another scab on my chin after yesterday's handstand disaster.)

"Don't I *always* look after you?" says Rose Rouge, stopping dead and pretending to be hurt. "Cross my hearts and hope to die?"

With her pinkie, she traces two tiny crosses over the interlinked pair of hearts dangling from the silver chain around her neck.

It's a twin to mine; the Luckenbooth necklace she bought me for ever ago. ("One heart is mine, one heart is yours," she'd told me the first time she fastened it around my neck.)

"Yes, you *always* look out for me, Rose," I tell her, reaching over and poking my stick back into the marshmallow bag, in the hope of spearing another pink blob. "What you *don't* always do is tell me when you're coming home!"

"Yeah, yeah . . . but I know you like secrets and surprises. It's much more fun just to show up here and bug you, instead of giving you three weeks' notice!"

She's started walking again, tossing her waist-length tangles of tinkling hair back off her face.

I swear, if anyone caught a glimpse of her through the trees and heard those tiny bells jingling, they'd think the Queen of the Fairies was passing by. OK, the Queen of the Freaky Fairies maybe. . .

And who knows what any stray, sensible Saturday morning wood-strollers would think of me? I don't suppose it's every day that you see a (nearly) thirteen-year-old girl wandering through the Scots pines wearing a Hawaiian garland made out of genuine plastic flowers around her neck. But how could I *not* wear it, when it was a present from Rose Rouge? (She always brings me presents when she comes; the cheaper and kitsch-er the better.)

"So, where were you last night? I wanted to talk to you," I tell her.

I'd wanted to spill the beans about my humiliating handstand. I'd wanted her to tell me how I could ever look Kyle in the eye again after that, but she hadn't got back to me.

"Last night?"

Rose Rouge scrunches up her nose as she thinks and *still* looks gorgeous. It's funny; me and her, we do look the same, sort of (big green eyes, snub noses, fat apple-y cheeks), but somehow Rose's combination looks amazing while mine looks stunningly nothing-to-go-wow-about.

"Yeah, last night," I prompt her. "You can think

back that far, can't you? Don't tell me you're going senile already!"

"*Cheeky!*" she grins, lobbing a marshmallow at my head and missing. (Hope some woodland creature enjoys that later on.) "I just can't remember. . . Oh, hold on; yeah – *that's* right! Me and my friends were helping this guy in our class with his latest art project!"

Urgh . . . that suddenly reminds me that Ms McIver, our art teacher, set us an assignment that I'd tucked into a dusty, cobwebby, faraway corner of my mind and forgotten about. If she asked me about it in her class on Tuesday, I'd just have to say it was going to be a surprise (i.e. a surprise to *me* as well as *her*, since I hadn't a clue what to do).

"So what was your friend's project like?"

Hey, maybe I could get inspired.

"It's about the human body. We all had to wear these stupid costumes he got for us, then we covered each other in paint and chucked ourselves at this *huuuge* canvas!"

Hey, maybe I *wouldn't* be getting inspired after all.

"I was in a tutu, and I was blue – see?"

Rose grabs a handful of dreadlocks and shows me the evidence; blue paint in the tips of her hair that obviously didn't wash off in the shower.

"Mmm . . . looks kind of nice," I tell her. "But

y'know, *I'm* a bit stuck over a project at school. Our teacher wants us to do some artwork for the entrance hall of the school, in time for the parents' night that is coming up. Got any ideas that don't involve me rolling in paint in a tutu or gorilla suit or something?"

Rose Rouge thinks for a second, then fires some suggestions my way.

"How about . . . a drawing of your school?"

"Too boring."

"A *model* of your school, made out of sardine cans, then?"

"Too complicated. And smelly."

"A self-portrait, carved out of a pumpkin?"

"Too silly."

"A self-portrait made out of marshmallows?"

"Too squashy. *And* silly."

"A collage of the Craigandarroch Lodge?"

"Too. . ."

I stop when I realize that the rest of that comment is ". . .perfect".

Rose Rouge takes my silence to be a good sign and carries on waffling.

"You could make the collage out of stuff you find right around here, Lemmie, like flowers and leaves and whatever. Bits of bark would be good for the tiles on the roof, and lichen would be great for the ivy creeping all over it!"

Craigandarroch Lodge is just there, in all its faded, boarded-up glory, the chinks of mica in the grey granite blocks making it shine and twinkle through the dark pines and darker rhododendron bushes. No one's lived in the place in fifty years, apart from whole dynasties of spiders and slugs and stuff. But from a distance – if you try not to notice the boards nailed across the windows – it still tries to look as fancy-pants grand as it once was, with its towering turrets and swirly-whirly curlicues. (That's posh for bendy bits of buildings, like wedding-cake icing, in case you were wondering.)

"Here!" says Rose Rouge, tipping out what's left in the rustly bag she's holding (three pink marshmallows, four white). "Let's start gathering stuff now!"

And so we do. Even though I don't know what I'll use them for yet, I gather up chunks of heather and bunches of clover, and dump them in the plastic bag. Rose Rouge comes back with bark and moss and the most beautiful coiled and unfurling ferns.

When the bag is full to bursting, me and Rose – bunches of ferns in our hands – go and stand on the waist-deep weed-fest that was once a long-ago perfectly mown lawn in front of the Lodge.

"Brilliant!" sighs Rose Rouge.

"Yeah, brilliant."

"This'll make such a good project, Lemmie!"

"Yeah, I know," I say, feeling like Rose Rouge's mini-me and not caring a bit.

A tiny someone in my head puts their hand up to remind me that I haven't spoken to Rose yet about Kyle. But it's funny, when I'm with Rose Rouge, nothing seems to matter as much as it did. . .

"Shh . . . is that a *deer*?" whispers Rose, whipping her head around to see a rustle of leaves that *might* have been a deer in the shadows of the woods at the other side of the looky-likey "lawn".

"Maybe," I tell her, though I'm not looking in the same direction.

Instead, I'm staring at the kaleidoscope of colour and shapes that make up Rose Rouge.

Now that all my bad memories and bad dreams are fading away – like they happened in a different life, to a different girl – I guess I don't need to rely on her so much any more. But there's one thing I couldn't bear to fade away, and that's Rose Rouge.

"Last one to the front door of the Lodge is a smelly kipper!" Rose Rouge calls out suddenly, grinning over her shoulder at me as she starts bounding over the wildflowers and grasses before I know it.

"Cheat!" I yell after her, all mumfy, maudlin thoughts pushed out of my mind as I race to catch up and prove that I'm no smelly kipper. . .

5

Sun, rain and mild freakiness

Q: Is "Isla"...

a) A bit like "island", only the end of it's floated off?

b) The name of a glen in Scotland?

c) The name of my gran?

d) The tiny doll dangling from a nail outside my room?

A: All four. (Sorry ... trick questions are *so* annoying, aren't they?)

"Night, night, Isla," I say, kissing my finger and then touching Isla's tiny cloth face with it.

Everyone should have a door angel.

It helps you sleep better when you know someone's guarding your room. And same when you're out – a door angel keeps all your personal, special stuff safe.

Course Isla wasn't *always* a door angel. For a long time, she was just a regular doll, given to me by my gran (who Isla is named after) when I was little.

"Isn't she the cutest thing? She's only the size of my hand!" Granny said to me at the time, sounding more enthusiastic about the little rag doll with the red plaits than I was at first. (I'd wanted a Ninja Turtle – my parents have never been keen on pets and I thought it would be the closest I'd get to one.)

But I did grow to love Isla, specially when I realized she was soft and squashy and small enough to stuff in a pocket and take with me wherever I went.

And then there was the time when I got too old to be carrying a doll around, as a certain someone at my primary school kindly pointed out to me by trying to flush Isla down the loo. After I brought Isla home dripping wet and smelling of Domestos, Rose Rouge suggested I give her a promotion to door angel. All it took was to sew a little bit of pink ribbon on her back and hammer a small nail into the doorframe to hang her from.

Isla's been in her job for about four years now; three of them guarding my big, high-ceilinged, barn of a bedroom back in Edinburgh, and one taking care of my slightly tilted, tiny attic room here in Balgownie.

By the way, I'm all on my own again (not counting Isla). It's about half-nine on Sunday night, and Rose Rouge is long, long gone. She didn't even stay for breakfast this morning – she threw her baggy polka-dot pyjamas and pink toothbrush into her homemade patchwork bag and took off for the bus back to Edinburgh before Mum and Dad were awake.

She might have sneaked out before even *I* was awake, if I hadn't heard her scrabbling around for her rings and things on the floor.

"Are you leaving already?" I'd mumbled, still more than half-asleep.

Me and Rose Rouge, we'd had our walk in Craigandarroch woods yesterday, and we'd had fun after that looking through all the stuff we'd gathered for my collage. We'd eaten our tea like a picnic on the floor of my room, sung along to our favourite CDs, and done impressions of people we knew (I did Jade telling a joke badly, Rose did a guy from art school who gets hiccups whenever they have to draw a nude model in their Life Drawing class).

But all that wasn't enough; I was still greedy for more time with Rose. I hadn't even had a chance to speak to her about Kyle yet.

"Got to go, peanut!" Rose Rouge had grinned at

me, leaning over and ruffling my already sleep-ruffled hair, with a jangle and clank of bracelets. "You're not the only one with homework and projects to do, y'know!"

When she waved bye from the bedroom door, the early morning sunshine twinkled on the chunky silver-heart rings she wears on her hand.

I lay in bed for ages after that, partly because my room is a nice place to be in the morning (specially when the sun's spangling through the skylight window like that), and partly 'cause I was still washed-out from last night's bad dream.

Recurring: that's what you say when you get a dream more than once. Well, I don't know how many times I had the dream when I lived in Edinburgh, all I know is that it still cropped up for a while when we moved here. I hadn't had it for months, till the early hours of last night, when I suddenly found myself sucked back into my old classroom, with Sammi and Carys and Nicola and everyone all snarling and sniggering at me like a pack of hyenas, till I shrank smaller and smaller and smaller like Alice in Wonderland, and all I could see above me was a circle of blurred, manic faces. And then that one, sugar-sweet voice drifted in, cheerfully announcing, "See, I *told* you – Laurel Ferguson is just a total freak!"

"FREAK!" yelled Sammi and Carys and Nicola and whoever else was in that mean cluster of faces, egged on by that certain sugar-voiced someone. "FREAK! FREAK! FREAK—"

"Night, Laurel!" Mum's voice drifts up from the bottom of the stairs.

"Night, Mum!" I call back down, shaking off the memory of the dream, closing the door on Isla and walking into my room. Then something makes me stop, and I reach out and unhook Isla from her nail, and stick her in my shirt pocket, just like old times.

"Want to help me find the perfect spot for my genuine plastic Hawaiian garland?" I ask her.

Two dark dots of knotted-thread eyes stare back up at me.

"Actually, its proper name is a 'lei'. That's what Rose Rouge told me," I explain. "Hawaiian islanders put them around the necks of visitors to welcome them."

A proper Hawaiian lei is made from fresh orchids or exotic tropical blooms, that's what Rose Rouge said. My Scottish lei, bought from one of those corny Pound stores (i.e. everything's £1, unless it's not), is made from the sort of blue plastic flowers you're never going to see anywhere but in a cartoon.

"Maybe I could pin it around one of the skylight

windows?" I ask Isla. "But then I kind of like those the way they are."

One of the skylights has got fairy lights that look like miniature Japanese lanterns wrapped around it, the other one's got a string of red chilli-pepper fairy lights draped over it.

I glance around my very small room, looking for inspiration. But somehow last night's dream keeps lapping up to the edges of my thoughts.

"Hey . . . do you want to hear a bedtime story?" I say distractedly to Isla, as I wander around, trying the lei here and there for size.

Isla says nothing, which I take as a yes.

"Well, once upon a time, there were four little girls who were the best of friends," I begin to tell her. "They played and laughed together all day long, and had lots of fun. Then one day, a beautiful princess turned up and said she wanted to be friends too. Three of the little girls were happy to have another playmate, but the fourth had a funny feeling that something wasn't right – she'd guessed that the beautiful princess was really a wicked witch in disguise. . ."

Isla listens intently, gazing up at me from the safety of my pocket.

"The witch soon realized that she'd been spotted, and cast a spell over the three little girls and everyone else, so they all thought the witch was still a beautiful princess, and that the fourth little girl was just a strange, mad, bad person that they shouldn't talk to or play with again. The End."

Hey, it's not a very good story. It's not the sort of story that's going to score me high points in my English class. The sad thing is, it's true; the sad thing is the fourth little girl was me, and the wicked witch was—

Oh, wow.

I mean, *wow*. . .

Rose Rouge always says that part of marshmallow magic is learning to read signs. And right now, outside the chilli-pepper window, the whole of the sky seems to be trying to tell me something. Something *important*, by the look of it.

With a creak and a push, I get the stiff skylight open. I stare out and breathe in, smelling grass and heather and heat and rain all at the same time.

Straight ahead, past the rooftops of the town, over by the faraway Glentorran mountains, the early summer evening sun is slithering down, all soft-slipping shades of orange and pink.

But coming from the right of me, over the top of Craigandarroch hill, is a gang of bruised deep-purple and steel-grey clouds, clattering together in a roar of thunder and crash of lightning.

If *that* wasn't enough, there's a rainbow hovering

hazily in the north-west, somewhere near the Tor-na-dee ski slopes, and the faintest hint of moon is already glowing right above my head.

"Y'know, I think it *is* a sign!" I whisper to no one at all, getting shivers prickling along the length of my spine as the storm cloud races over the top of the slate roof tiles of my house and splatters me with fat, heavy raindrops.

So I've worked out it's some spooky kind of sign. (I've also worked out that I'm getting wet, but it's kind of fun and exciting and better than remembering dreams you don't want to remember.) But a sign for *what* exactly?

Thirty seconds later, I'm perched halfway out of the window, with cool rain drenching my face, only now with my Hawaiian lei draped round my neck for luck and grinning like an idiot.

A clash of weather; I'm sure that's supposed to mean big changes are on the way! I think to myself, trying to be a good student and remember all the marshmallow magic Rose Rouge taught me, as the raindrops collect on my eyelashes.

Ker-*ASHHHHHHH*!!

Uh-oh, that streak of lightning was horribly close.

One thing's for sure; I don't want the change to be *me* made of flesh and blood one minute, and just a pile of ashes the next.

Time to get indoors, I think, and wait for tomorrow, when I might find out what this particular sweet gloop of marshmallow magic means. . .

6

Greetings from Planet Polka-dot

One.

Give me a one.

Or a three – a three would be good. 'Cause three equals a *whoo-hoo!* day, and who could resist a *whoo-hoo!* day? The last time I rolled a three and got a *whoo-hoo!* day, I found a five-pound note I thought I'd lost in the pocket of my dressing gown. (And no, I can't figure out why I'd put it there either. I mean, how often do you need to take money with you when you're going from your room to the shower?)

OK, so all that might sound a bit confusing. But then I woke up confused. First, because I thought I heard a scrabbling, and convinced myself Rose Rouge was here in the room with me again (she wasn't; I'd just been dreaming my bad dream again), and second, because I was confused and excited to see what big changes were on the way, after last night's weird weather.

That's what made me decide something: before I did the usual Monday morning stuff (staring at my clothes wondering what to wear; panicking that I hadn't done all the homework I was meant to do over the weekend; trying to make my hair sit not funny; go down to breakfast), I would do a smidgen of marshmallow magic that I hadn't tried in ages.

Course, *now* I could tell you what all the different sides represent in Roll of the Dice *backwards*. But I still like to open up the well-worn, folded scrap of paper Rose Rouge scribbled the meanings on originally – it's as if that's part of the magic too. (Her writing's so like mine, only prettier and more artistic, like me and her, really.)

So as I shake the white plastic dice in my hand – wishing hard for one dot or three dots to appear face up when I chuck it – I cast my eyes over Rose's purple-penned list.

If the dice lands on:
1 = Expect an ace day
2 = Expect an averagely OK day
3 = Expect a whoo-hoo! *day*

4 = Expect a work-a-delic day
5 = Expect a charmed day
6 = Expect the unexpected
And so I *chuck*. . .

Right – it's rolling, and now it's stopping. It's stopping on. . .

Six!

So I should expect the unexpected? I guess that's OK; it kind of fits in with last night's signs and everything.

Now I'll just have to be patient (that'll be easy – not!) and wait to see what happens next. . .

"Laurel! Breakfast's ready!"

Er, *after* I've had my breakfast, I mean.

Dad might be pretending to look through the mail, but the fingers of one hand are creeping across the table towards my plate.

"Gerroff!" I giggle, hitting his hand with my piece of peanut-butter toast.

"Aww, can't I have the other half of your toast? Don't you love your old dad?"

I do love my dad, who isn't very old actually, but he's still not getting my toast. It's not *my* fault he's bored of his dull-as-sawdust muesli.

"Get your own peanut-butter toast!" I tell him.

"Can't. I'm into healthy eating, remember? You don't want to be seen out with some big, fat father, do you?!"

As well as not being old, dad's not fat either – like Mum, he's into the whole healthy, perfect-image thing. But then you can't exactly go and see clients and persuade them that you know all about fancy, cutting-edge design if you look like a pair of slobs in old tracksuit bottoms with matching beer bellies, I s'pose.

"All the more for me, then!" I joke, pulling the jar of peanut butter closer to me.

I like joking around with Mum and Dad. When they haven't got their heads lost in a whirl of stainless-steel worktops and Welsh limestone flooring (which is a *lot* of the time), they can be good fun. Even when me and my parents seem like we come from two different planets (*them* from the Planet Beige, *me* from the Planet Polka-dot), we get on pretty well. Maybe they don't particularly like it or understand it, but Mum and Dad have always been pretty good about letting me dress the way I want to, or decorate my bedrooms how I've fancied. (Shonagh Robertson in my class says her mum won't even let her take down the *Little Mermaid* borders that've been in her room since she was four, let alone put up posters from *Smash Hits*.)

There are only *three* things about my parents that are a pain, and that's:

1) They don't approve of pets (too messy).

2) They've always worked so hard at their business that we don't get to just hang out often enough.

3) They don't approve of anything superstitious (which is why the only bit of marshmallow magic they know about is Isla).

"D'you want a yoghurt this morning, Laurel?" Mum asks me, as she grabs a carton for herself out of our huge American-style fridge (you could keep a small herd of deer in there and still have room for a family-size load of shopping from Sainsbury's).

"No, I'm fine with just toast today."

Mum is trying to be subtle, but I can tell she's checking out my outfit. I know she's just itching to do a minimal makeover on me, just like her and Dad did on practically our whole house. She'll approve of the shirt (denim-look, with short puff sleeves), 'cause she bought it for me. It's just the rest of it that's probably giving her a migraine.

But as Rose Rouge would say: *tough*.

I happen to *like* my pink shell top with the red cowgirl on, and my patterned, pale green, surfer-chick cut-offs. (Not that I get to do a lot of surfing in the middle of the Scottish Highlands, as you might have guessed. . .)

"Is that new?" Mum says casually, nodding at my hand-made bracelet, made out of pink ribbon and a stray plastic blue flower that fell off my Hawaiian lei last night. She really means, "What's that bit of tat wrapped round your wrist?", but she's too polite to say so.

"Mmm. . ." I mumble through a mouthful of toast.

"Looks cool, Laurel!"

Urgh. I wish Dad wouldn't do that.

Don't you just *squirm* when parents use the word "cool"?

I mean, I know that my parents are quite trendy and everything (they wear a lot of neat-pressed Gap stuff, compared to Morven's parents who live in fleeces, old jeans and hill-walking boots, and Jade's, who both work in offices and wear dull suits).

And I *know* what my parents do for a living sounds pretty trendy too, if you compare their jobs to Morven's mum and dad (farmers), or Jade's (they both work in the bank).

Still, my dad *might* have a haircut like Liam Gallagher once had, but that does NOT mean he can go using words that are only suitable for people under the age of sixteen. (When Morven was last round, he said her new mini-disc player was "wicked". I nearly *died* of shame. . .)

"Hey – got something to show you, Laurel!" Dad waffles on, oblivious to my cringing. "Wait till you see this!"

Mum winks at me, as Dad disappears into their office – which is right next door to the kitchen – then pops back again, holding his huge A3 drawing pad in his hands.

"What is it?"

As I ask, I brush the crumbs off my chin and then tuck my hands out of sight. If I didn't already have a middle name, then it'd have to be "Clumsy". The last thing I want to do is get greasy fingerprints over Dad's latest design.

"Your room, Laurel. Well, your *new* room, once the builders are finished knocking down the ceiling and wall and putting the dormer in. *And* once we get it decorated. Your mum sourced these paint colours from this really cool outlet in Glasgow –"

Oh, no . . . not this again. Was *this* the big change that last night's weather meant? I'd hoped Mum and Dad had gone off the whole idea of tearing out and re-building my room. They hadn't mentioned it for months.

"These shades of paint – they're a bit like what you've got now, Laurel," Mum jumps in. "Only more muted and soft!"

Y'mean pastel and bleurgh! I think.

"But I don't *want* my room changed! I've told you that already; I *like* it the way it is!"

Me and Rose Rouge; neither of us really get why Mum and Dad decided to buy an old-fashioned cottagey style house in Balgownie, and then went all hyper-modern inside, thumping down walls and extending it and turning the whole ground floor into what looks like a very posh, plush dental surgery.

The only bit of the house that isn't all sleek-chic and minimal is up in the attic (i.e. my room), where everything's more junk-chic and *max*imal. But that's the way I like it, and so does Rose Rouge, which is why she sleeps on a pile of cushions on the floor next to me when she comes to stay, rather than the cold, streamlined spare room downstairs.

"But it's so *small* up there, Laurel!" says Dad, looking as shocked as if I'd just announced I was chucking in school and joining the Navy.

"I *like* it small!" I hear myself protest, as I drop my toast on to the plate now that my parents have made me lose my appetite.

"Laurel, we can't exactly do up the whole house and then leave the upstairs untouched!"

When Mum says that, I feel a tidal wave of *aaaaaRRRGHHH!* rising in my chest.

"You . . . you both think that things that *don't*

matter matter a *lot* – but the things that *do* matter, you don't seem to think they do! *Matter*, I mean!"

And with that burbled little speech, I go and grab my bag and stomp out of the front door and off to school.

Y'know, I'd like to say, hey, *that* told my parents. But I have a horrible feeling my burblings made more sense in my head than when they tumbled out of my mouth just now.

I've suddenly got this sinking feeling that instead of looking at each other and admitting that I have a point, my parents are probably shaking their heads and wondering if a passing spaceship swapped me with their own child at birth. I bet they're imagining the *real* Laurel Ferguson – dressed in a cream hooded top and a nice beige skirt – living with a family of one-eyed, three-nosed, tartan-coloured aliens somewhere on a polka-dot planet.

Actually, can I get beamed up there right now? Everything might make a *lot* more sense. . .

7

N.U.T.T.E.R. spells "Lemmie"...

An ice-pole: that's not a big pointy stick you find frozen in the ground at the North Pole, surrounded by curious penguins and an mildly intrigued polar bear, in case you were wondering.

Instead, it's what we in Scotland call one of those long, thin tubes of icicle you can buy for not very many pence, when there's no way you can afford a Cornetto.

And thanks to having not very many pence indeed, me, Morven and Jade had just one (extra-long) ice-pole between us. Cola-flavoured, to be precise.

"I still can't believe I got *eight* out of fifty. . ." Morven moans miserably.

"I'm just glad I passed," I say, relieved to have

heard I got more-than-half of the questions right when Mrs Fraser gave us our French test results earlier.

Jade isn't saying anything, but that's because she got forty-eight out of fifty and probably doesn't want to rub our noses in it. Or maybe it's 'cause it's her turn to suck on the ice-pole.

"And you passed thanks to your marshmallow magic, didn't you, Lem?"

"Yep," I nod at Morven, as I silently thank my fossil for keeping me calm enough to concentrate on Friday.

"So . . . what about that sign you saw in the weather last night?" Morven asks me now. "What do you think'll happen?"

"Like I already said, I don't know. I'll just have to wait and see."

"What about *those* clouds, Lemmie? What are they saying?"

"Huh?"

"I just mean, what are the clouds telling you, by their shapes and, er, everything?"

Sometimes Morven can be a bit dippy. It doesn't matter how much I try to explain marshmallow magic to her, she never quite gets it.

"They're not telling me anything," I shrug, tilting my head back and gazing up at the general wispiness in the blue sky above us, and twirling today's feather (a magpie's) between my fingertips.

It's Monday, it's after school, we're hanging out on one of the benches in the town square, and for the last five minutes on and off I've been trying to explain about the signs for change I saw in last night's screwy weather. Like I say, I don't think Morven understands. I think Jade *might*, but she's gone a bit quiet, sucking on the ice-pole and not really saying anything much about anything. (What's she thinking? That I'm slightly psychic? Or that I'm as screwy as last night's weather?)

"They're cirrus."

"They're whatty?" Morven swirls her head around to ask Jade, who's finally said something at last. "What does 'cirrissus' mean?"

"*Cirrus*. And it doesn't *mean* anything," says Jade, passing her extra-long ice-pole to me. "It's just the name of the type of cloud. If it's wispy like pulled-apart candyfloss, then it's cirrus."

"Oh," says Morven, blinking hard and sounding just as confused by Jade's geographical weather definitions as by my spooky, weirdy-beardy sign-spotting burbles.

The three of us stare up at the candyfloss wisps and are happily silent for a few seconds, the way only best friends can be. Then for half a second, I feel the faintest flutter of panic. What if everything changes? What if Jade and Morven stop wanting to be friends with me? It's not such a dumb idea: after all, I used to feel this comfortable with Sammi and Carys and Nicola. The four of us were inseparable, till the wicked witch came along.

"Hey, I totally forgot to say, Lemmie," Morven bursts into the silence (and my panic) all of a sudden, "were you walking in the woods on Saturday, around lunchtime? Near Craigandarroch Lodge?"

"Uh . . . yeah. I was there. With Rose Rouge."

I'm all tongue-tied. Somehow it feels weird to have been watched and not know it, even when the person doing the watching is one of my best friends.

"Omigod, it *was* you!" gasps Morven. "I was there with Dad and Callum! I thought I saw you through the trees, but you were really far away. Were you wearing a red top or something?"

"No, oh no," I say, shaking my head. "That was Rose Rouge. She was wearing this amazing velvet dress that I think she got in some hippy shop in Edinburgh. . ."

"Wow! If I'd known you were with her, I'd have shouted after you. Or got Dad to shout – he's much louder than me. I can't believe I was *that* close to meeting your sister at last!"

"Next time, I *promise*," I tell Morven, and for that

matter, Jade. "I just didn't know she was going to be here. But next time she visits, I'll call you both for sure, and we can meet up."

I'm not sure I'm telling the truth. Like I say, I'm happier keeping Rose Rouge to myself.

"We could take her round to the café – show her off!" Morven suggests.

She means the café that's just round the corner from us now; it's where the whole of the town's school population drifts in and out, except in the height of summer, when the tourists take over.

"Or *maybe*," says Jade, "during the holidays, the three of us could get the bus down to Edinburgh and visit your sister for the day?"

"Mmmm!"

I know my mumble sounds vague, but it's got less to do with Rose Rouge and more to do with the idea of being back in Edinburgh. Amazing as the city is, I've got a few too bad memories of living there, memories that I like to keep locked in a dark cupboard at the back of my mind.

Anyway, I like being here in Balgownie. I love everything about this town, from the hills and woodland walks all around it, to the sparrows, eagles and hang-gliders that swoop over it, to the deer and the rabbits and the salmon that trot, hop and leap in front of me when I least expect it.

And then – of course – there're the brilliant friends I've made here, and I've got to say hurrah (mad as it might sound) for my school and the teachers, especially my art teacher, Ms McIver. That might sound like sucking-up, but honestly, you'd definitely *never* hear me droning on happily about my *last* school in Edinburgh (Sunnybank) or my favourite teacher there (Mrs O'Farrell for a while, till I realized she wasn't ever going to be on my side. . .).

Y'know, I've just realized something. I don't ever have to go back to Edinburgh. I don't ever have to think about what went on at my old school. Sammi and Carys and Nicola are history, and what happened with them isn't going to happen with Jade and Morven – I've just got to keep reminding myself of that. And reminding myself that I deserve to be happy.

"Lemmie – what are you doing?"

What I'm doing is getting up and standing on the bench, arms outstretched.

"I'm just letting everyone know I'm happy! H.A.P.P.YYYYYY!!" I yell, to anyone – including Jade, who asked the question – who happens to be listening.

And that –

(uh-oh)

– seems to include Kyle Strachan and his mates,

Jack McLennan and Iain Whyte, who are on the other side of the road, grinning like crazy.

"You are a N.U.T.T.E.R., Lemmie Ferguson!" Jack shouts over in my direction. His grin tells me he means that in a funny way rather than a nasty way. (I hope.)

But due to the shock of being caught looking like a deranged fruitcake, I automatically let go of the ice-pole I've still been holding, and it lands smack on Morven's neck, and slithers down the inside of her T-shirt.

"EEEEEEEKKKKKKKKK!"

On the other side of the road, Kyle, Jack and Iain are now doubled over laughing.

On *this* side of the road, me, Morv and Jade are mortified, but are hit by a dose of the giggles too.

"Give me that!" sniggers Jade, trying to snatch the ice-pole that Morven's wrestling from inside her top like it's a venomous snake or something. "And *you* – get down!"

She's speaking to me, tugging at the bum of my trousers, trying to get me off the bench before I can make more of a fool of myself – and my mates – than I already have.

But as it happens, I'm truly *excellent* at making a fool of myself, and I instantly do it again.

"What, are you playing at statues now, Lem?" asks

Jade, noticing that I'm frozen to the spot, going nowhere fast.

I can't answer. Not only has my mouth lost the power of speech, but my brain has lost the power of thinking. It's not the sight of Kyle Strachan that's left me perched on the bench like this; it's the posh car that I've just seen parking on the High Street. OK, so it's not so much the car as who's getting out of it. I don't mean the beardy bloke, or the flashily dressed blonde-haired woman. It's the girl.

Omigod, *please* don't let it be who I think it is. . .

"Are you all right, Lemmie?" Morven's voice drifts up to me. "You look like you've seen a ghost!"

She's not a ghost. From this far away, I'm not even a hundred percent sure she is who I dread she might be. All I know is the very sight of that lookalike girl has made something flash into my head in Technicolour and Surround Sound.

Expect the unexpected.

That's what the Roll of the Dice told me this morning.

I just hadn't expected to see an ordinary, pretty girl in a ponytail who just for a second there reminded me of a wicked witch I used to know. . .

8

Edible toes and small, furry secrets

There's a small, scratchy, wet tongue licking my little toe.

"Hey, Lemmie – it's Jade's birthday a week on Saturday," says Morven, flicking through her diary and stopping at the bright red felt-pen lettering that says JADE'S BIRTHDAY!!! in huge capitals, surrounded by stars. "Did you remember?"

"Er, no I didn't," I say, giggling and fidgeting.

The fidgeting just makes the small, scratchy wet tongue lick my little toe even more frantically. It tickles.

"Me neither. Wonder what I'll get her?" Morven says thoughtfully. "D'you fancy getting her a present together?"

The reason we can sit in art class and talk so openly about nearly forgetting Jade's birthday is that she's off sick with a tummy bug today.

"Yeah . . . maybe! Eeek!"

Y'know, it's very hard to concentrate on what Morven is saying, now that a tiny set of teeth has started nibbling at my foot.

"Well, hello, Harvey!" I say, bending over to sneak a peek under my desk at the phantom toe nibbler.

Harvey – who happens to be a Jack Russell that looks like it's been crossed with a Beanie Baby – stops attacking my foot long enough to gaze at me with his adorable, adoring puppy-dog eyes. His tiny tail and back leg are all bandaged with blue stretchy dressings (thanks to getting them trapped in a door) but he still tries to thump-thump his tail on the floor.

"He's not bugging you, is he, Lemmie?"

That's Ms McIver, crouching down on the opposite side of the desk from me and talking to me under the table.

"No! He's fine!"

Harvey's more than fine, he's great. I wish he could be in our art class every day, and not just now, when Ms McIver has to keep a close eye on him so he doesn't chew his bandage off, like he probably would do if he was left at home all day on his own.

In fact, I think it should be law that every school classroom should have a dog in it. I mean, how much fun would it be to have a Labrador or sheepdog or something bounding around with you in P.E.? Or a cute chihuahua choosing your desk to stretch out on during a dull science class? (Hmm – that last one's not such a good idea; our science teacher Mr Guthrie would probably suggest we dissect it. . .)

"Well, let me know if he gets on your wick."

"I will," I nod at my teacher, knowing that Harvey could never get on my wick. I don't even mind that he's now chewing the fabric flower on my pink flip-flop. Not having a pet of my own, I soak up every second I get with anyone else's, whether it's Harvey here, or Jade's dopey red setter (called Brick, 'cause he's the same colour and as thick as one), or Morven's little brother's guinea pigs (Alfie and Little Mo).

Ms McIver gives me a beaming smile under the table and then straightens up again. I go to straighten up too, but don't make a very good job of it.

"Ooooww!"

"Are you all right?" asks Morven.

"Kind of."

I'm lying and the whole class and Ms McIver know it – the fact that I'm rubbing my head is a bit of a giveaway.

"Ouch! You must've lost a few braincells there, Lemmie!" Ms McIver jokes, though she's looking a little bit concerned. She comes around the table – giving me a better nosey at her cute, new denim pedal-pushers with turn-ups – and examines my hair for any signs of squidgy brain-leakage.

"Hey, you should wear a crash helmet, Lemmie!" Danny Wilson shouts over, and gets everyone laughing, even me.

"And you should get a muzzle for that cheeky mouth of yours, Danny!" Ms McIver jokes back, getting everyone laughing even more, especially Danny.

This is why I love Ms McIver and her art class so much – it's just brilliant fun. Maybe it's that way 'cause Ms McIver is quite young, and dresses like she's still a student. Her being so laid-back makes you feel like you're hanging out, doing art with a friend. Or maybe she's just a great teacher; one who knows exactly how to get everyone really vibed-up and excited about her subject.

And of course, Harvey helps. It's a shame he's only here till his trapped-in-a-door back end heals. . .

"Yap! Yap! Yap! Yap!"

"Oh, no, we've been too noisy and set Harvey off again," sighs Ms McIver, her cool fingers still on my head. "Can someone pick him up and quieten him down, before we all get into trouble and I lose my job?"

There's a scuffle as twenty people rush to help, but being nearest me (and my edible toes), Morven is the one scrambling under the table to grab Harvey.

"Thanks, Morven. OK, Lemmie – it looks like you'll live!"

Ms McIver pats me on the shoulder, now that she's checked that I'm not injured or violating any Health & Safety rules by bleeding or oozing brain matter on to the classroom floor. Which is kind of funny really, since having a dog in a classroom is violating a Health & Safety rule or three. But we've all promised Ms McIver that we'll keep Harvey's presence a secret – just like everyone in all of her other classes. And since her classroom is in a Portakabin at the back of the playing fields where Mr Murray the headteacher can't be bothered to come, the chances of Harvey staying the art department's furry little secret are high.

"Right then," says Ms McIver, slapping her hands together. "Let's get started on our art projects today, shall we? I'm dying to see all your ideas. And parents' night is only a week and a half away, so we need to crack on fast!"

Normally there'd be loud screeches, clanks and chatter as everyone gets up to grab paper, paints and whatever, but today – at Ms McIver's request – we tiptoe around and chat low-level so that Harvey doesn't get too excitable and start his giveaway yap-yapping again.

"Thanks, Lemmie!" says Morven, as I place a bunch of art stuff in front of her. It's the least I can do, since Harvey has now crashed out, fast asleep and drooling happily, on her lap.

Now that Morven's sorted, I can get going on my own stuff. I've got a big piece of white card, some glue and my Boots carrier bag of woody goodies.

"Er . . . I hope you're not planning on doing any Body Art for this exhibition, Lemmie?"

I don't get what Ms McIver is saying at first; I haven't even emptied my plastic bag's worth of the leafy bits and planty bobs that I gathered with Rose Rouge at the weekend.

And then I notice that Ms McIver is pointing at my arms, at the green ink swirls around my freckles.

"Oh, I . . . I must have been sleepwalking last night!" I babble, wondering how I'd missed all those doodles in the shower this morning. "I only draw round my freckles when I sleepwalk!"

I haven't done that in months. But then I hadn't had my recurring dream in months either, and *that* was back.

"Don't you mean you sleep-*draw*?" Ms McIver

grins down at me, while everyone listens in and giggles. "And what made you sleep-draw last night, Lemmie? Was there anything in particular bothering you?"

Yes, there was something in particular bothering me last night; a memory of a familiar face that I *really* hoped I hadn't seen. I'd lain awake for ages persuading myself that I'd made a mistake, that it wasn't her.

I'm not about to tell Ms McIver that, though, because the bottom line is, I've never told anyone at my new school, in my new life – not even Morven and Jade – how bad things got back in Edinburgh. Because if I told them about the bullying, and the stuff I was supposed to have done, and being sent to the child psychologist, then they might back away from me, or *turn* on me, just like my old friends did. And then it would be like the wicked witch had won, all over again. . .

"Um . . . no, nothing's bothering me," I lie.

Morven's eyes are fixed on me, blinking faster than usual, and I can't help wondering if she knows I'm fibbing. Still, yesterday afternoon, her and Jade seemed to swallow my story about not feeling well. After leaping off the bench, I ran all the way to our house, only hesitating to run my fingers over the bark of every tree I passed on the way.

Why I needed to do the Tree-Touching – that protective bit of marshmallow magic – I didn't know. But Rose Rouge would.

Pity I couldn't get hold of her, then. And it was a pity too that none of the other marshmallow magic I tried on my own – holding the fossil, counting my feathers, sleeping with a piece of lucky rose quartz under my pillow – made my muddled head feel any better. In fact, I sneezed myself awake today with a feather fluttering at my nostrils, and for most of the morning I had an imprint of the rose quartz in my cheek after sleeping on it for hours on end (when I wasn't busy doodling on my arm. . .).

And before you ask, I rolled a six again today on the dice. It's only Day Two and I think I've already had enough of expecting the unexpected. . .

"Well, if you're *sure* nothing's bothering you, Lemmie," says Ms McIver, not sounding too convinced. "Anyway, what's all this stuff you've got here? This looks very intriguing!"

With a grin, Ms McIver picks up a piece of dried-out moss from my Boots bag and holds it to her top lip, like it's some fuzzy handlebar moustache.

Straightaway, everyone's nudging each other to look and having a snigger. I join in the sniggering, and that feels good – much better than fretting about sitting in the dark, drawing loop-the-loops round my freckles by the light of the moon, and knowing nothing about it.

All I can remember about last night is having weird dreams about girls ganging up on me and tippety-tappiting scuttling noises, neither of which I liked very much. Had my door angel been sleeping on the job? Isla really wasn't doing very well at keeping the bad dreams at bay. . .

"Lemmie?"

Oops.

I've been daydreaming about my nightmares and forgotten to answer Ms McIver's question.

"Um . . . I'm going to do a collage of Craigandarroch Lodge. We – I picked up all this stuff from the woods around there at the weekend."

"Fantastic!" says Ms McIver, putting down the moss and letting her fingertips investigate the surfaces of the rough bark, dotted fern leaves and bumpy pine cones I've brought along. "Have you got a sketch of the Lodge to work from?"

Oops (again).

I hadn't thought about doing a drawing of the place first, but it made more sense than trying to put this picture together from memory.

"I'm going to do that, I just haven't . . . yet," I waffle.

"Better hurry, then, Lemmie!" Danny Wilson calls

over cheerily. "They're just about to knock the place down!"

"Very funny!" I say back, pulling a face at Danny and sticking my tongue out at him.

"It's true, Lemmie!" Danny insists, taking his stupid teasing too far. "They're knocking down the Lodge and turning the whole place into a fancy health resort! My dad's company got the contract!"

It couldn't be true. The woods round Craigandarroch – that was me and Rose Rouge's favourite place to go, our special little world of sisterly chats, with the dark branches hanging all around us, keeping our secrets safe.

It couldn't be true. But Danny Wilson's dad was Balgownie's answer to Bob the Builder – he had a yard full of bulldozers and diggers and a team of people who knew how to use them.

It still couldn't be true, could it? But it must be, because Ms McIver is nodding and agreeing with Danny, and telling me that the demolition work is due to start any day now, it's been in the local paper and everything.

"Which makes your project very timely, Lemmie," I tune in to hear her say. "It's a way of marking a big changing point in Balgownie's local history!"

Changes . . . to think I'd got excited at the idea of that when I was watching the mad weather the other night. But all the changes I was hearing about seemed to be for the worse, like my parents still scheming to destroy my hidey-hole bedroom, and developers planning to destroy Craigandarroch.

"But why does everything have to change?" I ask out loud.

Too loud, as it happens. People around the room glance over at me, surprised by my outburst. I shudder slightly, remembering how everyone at Sunnybank regularly stared at me like I was a two-headed space alien dumped into their class.

"But things *always* change, Lemmie. Nothing ever stays the same!" says Ms McIver. "It's just the way of the world. *Que sera, sera!*"

I don't know what *que sera, sera* means, but I'm not about to ask because I've just felt a dark, heavy shape settle in my stomach.

"Look, he likes you!" says Morven softly.

I know she's trying to cheer me up, but even Harvey's scratchy puppy tongue licking my hand can't make me feel better right now.

Not when the shadow of the wicked witch keeps slipping into my sunshiney new world. . .

9

Just my Luck(enbooth)

Like I said before, Edinburgh is a very cool city.

You want a for instance?

Well, it has an amazing world-famous festival with music and comedy shows and street performers *every* summer – and it lasts for a whole *month*. And at New Year, there's a three-day party in the city centre, with fantastic fireworks ping-ponging from the towering castle that's right *plonk!* in the middle of town.

And that's not the only castle; there're two, at either end of the Royal Mile, a long road that's full of the most ancient buildings. The Royal Mile is where they first started selling Luckenbooths, way, way back in the 1700s. They were supposed to bring you luck in life and in love, and they were sold in booths.

(Hey, are you getting a clue how the name came about?)

Anyway, I was fiddling with the two intertwined hearts around my neck wondering when I'd get the chance to talk to Rose Rouge again, when I could tell her about Kyle, *or* the girl I sort of maybe recognized (and hoped I didn't) on Monday. And then I'd have to tell her the horrible news about Craigandarroch Lodge and the woods getting flattened. . .

"So do we have a volunteer . . . Lemmie Ferguson?"

And now it's Wednesday morning, and I'm about to be ritually humiliated by Mr Guthrie, our science teacher. He's quite entertaining in a loud, shouty way, but I wish he didn't think it was fun to volunteer me for every experiment going.

"Hummmmpphhh. . ."

"Now, then, Lemmie – no sighing!" Mr Guthrie booms, waving me up to join him. "The world of science needs brave souls like you!"

I don't feel very brave walking up to the front of the class, but at least everyone claps and cheers me on, like they always do. I give them a few jokey bows to say thank you and hear Morven giving me a girly "whoo-hoo!" of encouragement.

"Right!" says Mr Guthrie. "Let's talk a little about electricity today, shall we?"

Urgh. . . I don't know what's coming next, but I don't like the sound of that at *all*. Why does he always pick me? Maybe it's the way I dress – if I hadn't worn my new red denim skirt, stripy pink and blue cheesecloth shirt and my blue plastic flower bracelet wrapped round my ponytail, Mr Guthrie might not have noticed me. Maybe I should only wear nondescript grey when I come to his class, and sit at the back with a hood up. . .

"OK, Lemmie, if you just kick your shoes off, please, and take off anything metallic, like your watch, and your necklace."

What?!

Recently, Mr Guthrie has got me doing dumb stuff like racing against the clock to put a bunch of cubes in a box (something about the concept of speed); rolling a yoghurt pot around the room (angles and trajectory); and even pulling a handful of slimy pondweed out of a beaker (photosynthesis).

Cubes, yoghurt and smelly slime I can handle, but I don't want to be electrocuted. I don't even want to kick off my flip-flops, and I never *ever* take off my Luckenbooth. I promised Rose Rouge I'd always wear it, come rain, shine, or power-showers.

"Come on – chop, chop, Lemmie!" says Mr Guthrie, with the beaming enthusiasm of an executioner who loves his job too much.

What am I going to do? Mr Guthrie isn't going to understand that I can't take my necklace off 'cause it breaks a sacred bond with my sister. He doesn't understand anything that isn't pure science. He even took the mickey out of Jenna Harris for bringing in her lucky Pumba toy last month during a test. ("Superstitious twaddle," he'd teased her, picking up Pumba like he was contaminated. "You might as well have brought a lucky *potato* for all the help it'll give you!")

Can you imagine what he'd make of signs and charms and intertwined silver hearts that represent me and my sister? Can you imagine what he'd make of feathers and fossils and Tree-Touching?

And speaking of marshmallow magic, I think I need more than that to get me out of this. What I need is a full-on mira—

WHEEE-oooo. . . WHEEE-oooo. . . WHEEE-oooo. . . WHEEE-oooo. . .

—cle.

Wow.

"OK, everyone!" Mr Guthrie yells above the din of the fire alarm. "You know the score – leave bags and jackets where they are and file out towards the fire exit, *slowly*!"

"Thank you!" I whisper to whatever emergency angel just came to my rescue. . .

My hand is on my temple – pinkie extended – and I'm gazing glassy-eyed and wobbly-lipped at the woods beyond the garden.

"Oh, Papa! Verily, we are ruined! If the Lodge is gone, then all is lost! Mama and I will *surely* be sent to the poorhouse! Er . . . verily!"

"Nice try, Lemmie!" grins Jade, her arms folded across her chest. "It would be more convincing if you were wearing a Jane Austen type dress and not a denim skirt and flip-flops, though! And the digital camera round your neck – I'm not *totally* sure they had those in the 1800s. . ."

"Ah, well," I grin back at her, and turn to take a snap of the Craigandarroch Lodge, in all its faded, boarded-up glory.

"Let's see," says Jade, itching for a peek at the image on the mini-screen of my mum's camera. "That shot's great, Lemmie. It'll be really good to copy for your collage."

"Mmm . . . definitely," I say, looking up from the camera at the real thing. "But y'know I still can't get it into my head that this place is about to get bulldozed!"

Me and Jade, we're standing at the far end of the wildly overgrown lawn in front of the Lodge. Brick keeps disappearing into and bounding out of the long grass as he snaps hopelessly at lazily swooping dragonflies. He seems very pleased to be having an unexpected walk in the woods, thanks to the electrics going haywire at school and all of us getting the afternoon off. Which makes two of us. Actually, quite a *lot* of us, if you count the whole of Balgownie Academy – including the teachers, I bet.

"Yeah, it's a shame no one ever wanted to restore the place," says Jade, blinking back up at the Lodge. "But I guess it *is* a bit of a wreck. Still, so's my grandad and no one's trying to bulldoze *him*."

It takes a split-second and a grin from Jade to make me realize she's just (uh-oh) told one of her lousy jokes again.

"Very funny," I grin back, although it wasn't funny at all (sorry, Jade).

Jade missed the whole kerfuffle of the (false) fire alarm and the evacuation today. Even though she was feeling a lot better, her mum kept her off school again, "just to be on the safe side". Anyone else would think that was a bit of a result, but Jade – being Jade – was pretty gutted. (I'd call her a weirdo, but she's my mate.)

Anyway, with an afternoon stretching out in front of me with nothing to do, and a best friend in the shape of Morven deciding she'd rather take off with her mum to Tesco in her unexpected free time (yep, *another* weirdo!), I decided to come and photograph the Lodge for a) my art project and b) possibly the last time.

On the way to Craigandarroch, I'd dropped in at Jade's to see how she was doing. How she was doing was *borrrredddd*. With both her parents working at the bank, and her granny – who was meant to be keeping an eye on her – at the restaurant getting things ready for opening later, Jade didn't need much persuading to make a break for it and come with me for a walk in the woods. Along with Brick, of course.

"I wonder how Ms McIver got on when the alarm went off? She'll have had to smuggle Harvey out of the Portakabin!"

"She did!" I tell Jade. "She had him hidden behind a cheeseplant she'd brought in for the sixth years to draw in their Higher exam!"

I had a funny feeling Ms McIver might have looked more suspicious than she thought, hurrying over to her Mini Cooper during the fire alarm and stuffing a large houseplant in the passenger seat. Specially one that *yapped*.

It had been quite fun, that half-hour mooching in the school yard, while Mr Murray the head and Mr Thomson the caretaker ran around deciding what to do in the face of a non-emergency but an alarm system that didn't fancy switching off. Apart from people-watching, me and Morven and a few others got into cloud-gazing, battling to be the first to spot the stupidest-shaped cloud (I won, with a cloud that looked like a fluffy banana). A bunch of the boys – including Kyle Strachan – started up an impromptu football game using someone's lunch-pack apple, but I caught him smiling over once. I was showing some of the girls how I could make my kneecaps jerk up and down while Morven hummed the theme tune to *EastEnders* at the time, but I still think it was more of a smile than a snigger. (I hope.)

"Y'know, it's mad that the alarm went off, just when you were dreading that experiment," says Jade, bending over to pick a dandelion clock that's right at her feet.

Yeah, it *was* mad. But now that I'd had time to think about it, I wondered if it was a bit *more* than mad.

"I think Rose Rouge might have helped!"

At my words, Jade stands instantly up straight, dandelion clock clutched between her fingers.

"*How* exactly?"

The truth is, I don't know how exactly, but that's just marshmallow magic, isn't it? Couldn't the emergency angel have been sent by my sister?

"Well. . ." I shrug, not sure how to put it into words. "I tried to get in touch with Rose the last couple of nights, but she never got back to me. But then I think she might have somehow *known* I needed her help. I think she just . . . I dunno, sent some good vibes or something!"

Jade blinks at me. It's very hard to read her face; her dark almond eyes are giving nothing away and the rest of her face is . . . actually, what's that posh word for giving nothing away? Impassive – that's it. Jade's tiny and cute, like a little Chinese china doll, which makes some people treat her like she's younger than she is. But even though I'm quite a bit taller than her, when she blasts that look my way, I feel like *I'm* about five years old and *she's* old enough to have a mortgage and a husband and a law degree.

"Or maybe it just happened, Lemmie," she says, in a matter-of-fact voice. "Coincidences *do* happen."

I'm just about to tell her that Rose Rouge says coincidences are just a type of marshmallow magic, but then I shut up. I know Morven loves to hear me talk about Rose Rouge and the marshmallow magic and everything, but I'm not always sure Jade does. And this is one of those times.

"Um, speaking about coincidences . . . I meant to say, Lemmie," Jade suddenly says, as she twirls the dandelion clock between her thumb and forefinger, "when you ran off on Monday, from the Square, it wasn't just 'cause you felt ill, was it?"

"Course it was!" I laugh, feeling a cold drip of sweat slither from the top of my spine and meander its way down between my shoulder blades.

"Yeah, but what about those people getting out of the car on the High Street? I saw you watching them. . ."

I know Jade has vague plans to be a physiotherapist or a pilot when she's older, but I really don't think she should rule out being a detective.

For a second, I think about telling her she's got it all wrong, and then I realize I'd be wasting her time and mine.

"Well, I sort of thought I recognized them . . . the girl anyway," I tell her, with a shrug I hope looks casual. "From Edinburgh, I mean. She might have been someone from my old school, but it probably wasn't her."

The reason I was trying to sound so unbothered to Jade was that I was trying *really* hard to put the girl-who-reminded-me-of-you-know-who out of my mind. At least till I got the chance to speak to Rose Rouge about how muddled I'd felt since I saw her. And I'd been managing. *Not* to think about the girl-who-reminded-me-of-you-know-who, I mean. Except when I was sleeping, of course. It wasn't just my recurring dream, it was 'cause I'd woken up for the second day running with circles doodled round the freckles on my arm.

"Anyway," I continue, hoping I seem convincingly casual, "you said 'speaking about coincidences'. . .?"

"Well, yes. It's just that I think I saw that girl and her family again."

If I'd been wired up to one of those bleepy machines you get in *ER* right now, the wiggly electrical line of my heartbeat would have just *leapt* off the monitor screen.

"Oh, yeah? When? I mean, where?" I ask, trying to sound casual again.

It WASN'T her, I silently remind/convince myself again. *It was just some girl who looked a bit like her*. . .

I can't look Jade in the eye, 'cause she'll see for certain that I'm feeling about as casual as someone paddling in a pond full of piranhas. Instead, I drop my gaze to the dandelion clock she's still holding.

"Across the road from me. When I was bored yesterday, I went to look out my bedroom window, and I saw that same car parked outside that house opposite – the one that's let out for holidays."

I know the house she means – it has roses trained around the door and tartan curtains in the windows, all done out in twee cuteness for the tourists coming to stay.

"That girl and her parents; they were just going inside."

"Uh-huh. OK," I say, feeling a flurry of goose pimples flutter over my whole body. "So, that means they're just holidaymakers, then. Er . . . whoever they are."

Stop getting so freaked out – it WASN'T her! I shout silently at myself.

"I guess. . ." says Jade, her eyes still fixed on me.

Blaaaahhhh. . .

That how I feel; just *blaaaaahhhh* . . . like I'm a balloon that someone's just deflated. To cover the *blaaaahhhh* and the general confusion I feel, I do the first thing that comes into my mind.

"Are you using that?" I ask Jade, pointing to the dandelion clock.

"What?"

Jade is frowning her delicate, dark eyebrows into graceful arches.

"Can I use it then?" I say, not even trying to explain myself to her.

Jade is still frowning, as I lean forward and blow hard on the dandelion clock, sending the feathery tendrils flying off into the air.

Please don't let it be her . . . please don't let her

family have come here for a holiday – I couldn't stand it! I whisper in my head, as I blow hard and make a wish.

Thunk!

Brick has bounded over, coming to a standstill by using his furry head against Jade's back as a brake. Being jolted from behind by a dumb dog gets us both giggling, which is great – after all, Jade was probably just about to ask me what I wished for. . .

"C'mere!" Jade laughs, ruffling Brick's red, hairy head. "What have you got there, boy?"

"It's a toadstool! Or a mushroom," I say, bending down to look at it.

"Is it poisonous?" asks Jade, bending down to look too (only she doesn't have to bend so far).

"I don't know."

I haven't lived in the countryside long enough to figure out fungi. The only mushrooms I can recognize for sure are the ones in the vegetable aisle at the supermarket. We need farm-girl Morven to set us straight, but she's busy cruising round Tesco right now.

"Me neither," says Jade, who may be smart but obviously doesn't know her poisonous toadstools from her Chinese mushrooms (with bamboo shoots, *mmmm*. . .) either. "But we shouldn't let Brick eat it just in case. It could make him go mad or something!"

"Would you be able to tell the difference?" I say, looking down at Brick's dopily content face.

Giving my cheekiness just the quickest of grins, Jade starts ordering Brick to drop the mushroom. He doesn't. The more sternly Jade orders him, the more Brick looks up at her with adoring eyes, blissfully ignorant that she's trying to save him from potential death/illness/crazy-dom.

While she wrestles his jaws open and tries to shake the mushroom/toadstool out of his mouth, I suddenly spot where he got it from.

"Jade . . . omigod, I can't believe it!"

"What is it?" she asks, watching me walk off into the woods as she finally manages to get Brick to spit out the potentially poisonous whatever.

"It's a fairy circle!" I gasp, standing in the middle of an "o" of mushrooms/toadstools (give or take a space where one's been semi-eaten by a barking-mad red setter).

"What do you mean, fairy circle?"

Jade has just patted Brick softly on the rump, sending him off into the grass after dragonflies again.

"C'mere! Check it out, Jade!"

Yeah, I know Jade's kind of sensible and so's a bit funny about anything magical, but even she can't resist coming over to stand in the circle with me, staring around her at the (near) perfect circular swirl around our feet. And I can't resist trying to get her excited about it.

"It's really special to come across one of these!"

"Like how?" asks Jade, trying to sound cynical but still gawping at the domed little caps ringing our feet.

"'Cause it just *is*! And if you think it's lucky to make a wish on a dandelion clock or birthday candles, then it's a *zillion* times luckier to make a wish in a fairy circle!"

Hmm . . . maybe I shouldn't have given the example of the dandelion clock, since I'd just nicked that from her.

"What kind of a wish are you talking about?" says Jade, narrowing her eyes at me but at least not looking so cynical any more.

I already made the most important wish on the dandelion clock. Now it's time for my second most important wish.

"How about . . . how about we both make a wish that the Lodge and the woods don't get bulldozed?" I suggest. "Two people making a wish together is really, really . . . fun!"

"Two people making a wish together is really, really *powerful* marshmallow magic, that's what Rose Rouge always says," is what I *really* mean but I don't want to push it.

And not pushing it seems to have worked. There's a sparkle in Jade's normally sensible eyes that tells me she's up for this – even just for a laugh.

"OK," shrugs Jade. "So what do we have to do?"

"Well, first we have to hold hands . . . yeah, like that, then we have to close our eyes, and now we have to concentrate on wishing for—"

Well, we hadn't wished for a dog jumping into the charmed fairy circle – at least *I* hadn't – but that's exactly what's just happened.

"Gerroff, Brick!" I say, breaking into a shrieked giggle as Jade's dumb dog scrabbles his front paws on my chest and tries to lick a layer of skin off my face.

"Brick, *down*!" Jade orders him, as he transfers his licks from me to her.

Between me and Jade giggling and Brick happily "arrooooff!"ing, it would be hard to hear anything.

Except an ear-splitting, ominous crack of thunder directly above our heads. . .

Three pairs of eyes – mine, Jade's and Brick's – exchange laughing-yet-slightly-worried glances.

"Was that some sort of cosmic sign?" Jade smiles nervously.

"I dunno!" I tell her.

"Are the fairies annoyed 'cause my dog's eaten one of their toadstooly things and trampled on the rest?"

"I dunno!"

"Er, should we get out of here? Like, *now*?"

"Definitely!"

A red setter can run out of a wood very, *very* fast, but so can a couple of spooked-out schoolgirls, let me tell you. . .

10

ArTy, CrAfTy and shiny, shiny. . .

"ArTy. R-T. Aaaaargh-ty!"

As she strides by my desk, Ms McIver spots me gawping at the new artwork on the classroom wall – a muddle of different styles of multicoloured lettering – and smiles.

"Great, isn't it? A very clever play on words! It was done by one of the fourth years."

I nod, thinking how much Rose Rouge would like it. I'll have to tell her all about it, next time I speak to her, which will be *when*, exactly. . .?

"Shonagh! Can you do me a favour and stick the radio on?" says Ms McIver, moving off. "I feel like we need some music to get us all going today!"

I love the fact that Ms McIver lets us listen to the radio in class. I love that she doesn't mind at all if we chat, as long as we get on with our work. I love the fact that her puppy is making my toes tingle with his snoring.

"Hey, Lemmie!"

It's Jade, bending forward across the desk to see me past Morven. Her dark eyes seem to be staring a hole in my head.

"Are you all right after yesterday?"

Uh-oh. Jade must be talking about that bit of news she gave me when we were up by Craigandarroch Lodge; the news about the somebody/hopefully nobody family moving into the holiday cottage across the road from her. I've been trying very hard not to think about that. *Very* hard. Till now.

"...'cause my legs are *aching*, after running out of the woods so fast!"

Ah – Jade's not talking about that after all. She's talking about us racing the rainstorm home. And I don't suppose she's really staring at me so much as just plain old looking. She can't help the fact that she has the sort of intense gaze that can make you feel guilty, even when you haven't done anything.

"No, my legs are fine."

Actually, my legs might not be aching, but my toes are *definitely* vibrating.

"Morven, can you pass me that brush, please?" I ask, pointing to the thick, stubbly glue brush sitting in a jar close to her. "I, um, can't move to reach it because there's a dog asleep on my feet."

"Aww . . . isn't he just *gorgeous*?" Morven sighs, bending under the table to gawp at the snoozing Harvey and forgetting all about my brush. "Your shoes are like little velvet cushions for his head!"

I've got on red, velvet Chinese pumps today, with delicate embroidery of dragons and flowers sewn on each shoe (chosen for me by Rose Rouge, of course). The delicate embroidery and velvet will now have a layer of doggy hair on them, but I don't care. With every puppy-sized snore, Harvey's quivering head on my toes gives me the giggles.

"There – there's your brush," says Jade, passing it over Morven's bowed head. "I'm going over to the sinks. Need anything else brought back while I'm there?"

"Nope, I'm fine, thanks," I tell her, as I prop up my photo of Craigandarroch Lodge and start sticking more of the collage together. I did quite a lot of it at home last night, once Mum had run the photo out on the printer for me. For the glinting granite stones of the walls, I've used strips of bark from the silver birch trees dotted through the wall of pines in Craigandarroch wood. Broken-off sections of pine cone make up the roof tiles, small twigs outline the windows and drainpipes, and wispy bits of hair-moss trail as looky-likey ivy down the bark walls. All I need to finish the building is to decide what to do for the big circular window over the front door.

"What are you going to use for grass?" asks Morven, coming up for air after cooing over Harvey.

"Er, grass," I tell her, holding up a clear, plastic sandwich bag of the stuff. "I'll spread a lot of glue on and then just . . . *sprinkle*, I guess."

"I wish mine looked as good as yours. Mine's rotten. It looks like a caveman, doesn't it?"

The "it" is Morven's art project. She had been going to paint a bowl of fruit, but decided halfway through an orange that it was the most boring project in the world and asked Ms McIver if she could do something else. Ms McIver said fine, if she could do it in time, since there was just under a week till parents' night.

"No, it doesn't look like a caveman – it's great!" I tell her, nodding at the clay figure she's been modelling. It's quite cute, actually, with its squidgy face, blobs for hands and huge, knobbly knees.

"What's with the pro-wrestler, Morven?" Danny Wilson asks as he passes.

"Ignore him," I order my friend. "He's just trying

to wind you up. It does *not* look like a pro-wrestler!"

(Er, *there* was a bit of a white lie. Danny probably had a point.)

"Hmm. Of course I'm going to ignore him. Danny's an idiot. But I did want her to be prettier . . . a door angel should be pretty, shouldn't she?"

"And she *will* be!" I say, trying to inject a bit of enthusiasm into Morven, before she gives up on this as quickly as she gave up on the bowl of fruit. "Wait till you paint her and stick her wings on, then she'll be lovely!"

Morven blinks uncertainly at me, then a small smile starts to melt on to her worried face.

"Yeah, she will, won't she?" Morven agrees, picking up the piece of white netting that she's set aside for the angel wings and floaty skirt.

"And she'll look more of a proper door angel than *mine* – Isla's got no wings and is only dressed in a jumper and jeans!"

"Er . . . you really don't mind that I copied your door angel idea for my project, do you, Lem?"

"I told you before, I'm well chuffed that you think it's a good enough idea to copy! And hey, it wasn't my idea in the first place – it was Rose Rouge's, so *I* copied *her*!"

"You know," says Morven, suddenly looking intently at me. "You're such a nice friend, Lemmie.

It's like you always see . . . well, the *shiny* side to everything!"

The shiny side. Yeah, Rose Rouge has always told me to try and see the shiny side to everything, even the times when I've not been feeling too shiny *inside*.

"Thanks," I shrug, feeling chuffed and choked at Morven's compliment.

I want to tell her that she and Jade are pretty spectacularly nice too, but my voice is temporarily lost in a knot in my throat. Even just last period – in Computer Tech – Jade did a really sweet thing. When Miss Bachelor was busy trying to sort out how exactly Danny Wilson had managed to delete his entire work folder, Jade had sneaked on to the internet and looked up "sleepwalking". After waking up with another headful of strange scrabbling dreams and an armful of circled freckles this morning, she knew I'd been feeling like a freak again and searched some sites to find wildly weird stories of sleepwalkers just to make me feel more normal.

"Hey, Lemmie," she'd hissed across the table at me, "you've never gone for a wee in your wardrobe, have you?"

"What?" I squeaked back.

"That's what some people do in their sleep! No kidding – it says so here! And then there's a thing here about some guy in Germany who used to march along rooftops playing the tuba when he was sleepwalking. His neighbours must have *loved* him!"

Miss Bachelor had glanced over just then and given Jade one of those teacherly glowers that mean shut up, so that was the end of that. But at least Jade's dumb cheer-up efforts had worked and I felt a bit better – I mean, a few doodles did seem kind of tame compared to weeing in your wardrobe.

"I guess you must take after your sister," says Morven, turning back to her model and trying to squish the knees smaller. "Looking at things all shiny, I mean. From what you've said about her, anyway. . ."

Another compliment to make my cheeks glow. It's funny, but I never used to get compliments from anyone at my old school. At my old school I mostly just got stared at, slagged off or blanked.

Y'know, I don't even want to think about that. I'd rather talk about good stuff, shiny stuff, like Rose Rouge.

"Well, me and Rose are a bit alike, I guess," I tell Morven. "In fact we're practically identical, except for the fact that she's prettier and smarter and more *everything* than me!"

"Bet she's not," says Morven. "You're pretty pretty and smart and everything all by yourself!"

Morven's giving me the funniest little smile. I can't work out why it seems funny, but it's probably just me being paranoid and rubbish at accepting compliments. Specially when she keeps piling them on like she's doing.

"Hey, look what Rose sent me. . ." I say hurriedly, pulling something out of my jeans pocket.

I hadn't meant to show either of my friends this; I'd meant to keep it as a small secret something-and-nothing just for me. But now I really wanted Morven to see how special Rose Rouge is.

"A sweet?"

Morven is frowning at the Loveheart I'm holding.

"Well, yeah . . . but it's more what it says."

"*'YOU AND ME'*."

I can tell Morven doesn't quite get the message, but then she doesn't have a sister that she feels almost supernaturally close to. She's only got Callum, who picks fights with her over who's got the biggest pile of mashed potatoes and puts worms in her trainers for fun.

"It's just her way of saying we'll always be together," I try to explain. "Like my Luckenbooth. She'll always be there for me, y'know?"

"Yeah, but she *hasn't* been there for you, has she? You said she hasn't been in touch for days!"

Um . . . that's true, but it doesn't feel good to hear Morven say it, all blunt and brusque like that.

"But that's just Rose Rouge. . . She's doesn't *mean*

it. It's just that she's always madly busy, or off doing stuff or whatever. She probably doesn't even know what day it is. You know how wild she is!"

"Well, kind of. I mean, I remember you once said that she was pretty wild when she was at school. What did she get up to again?"

"Oh, stuff like. . ."

I wrack my brain, frantically searching for examples. It's the same when someone asks you what your favourite book is, or favourite movie, and in your mind the word "BLANK" flashes up in dayglo letters.

". . .oh, I know!"

As the rest of the class chats and the radio blares and Harvey snoozes, I tell Morven tales of Rose Rouge when she was younger, one story after another pinging into my head, after the first one tumbles out of my memory.

I tell her about the time Rose Rouge found a tiny, round antique pot at a car boot sale that had "Rose Rouge" on it in old-fashioned, swirly writing. When she opened it, inside the pot was a perfect dome of deep red powder blusher, unused by whoever had bought it however many decades ago. Blown away by the coincidence and inspired by the colour, Rose counted out her pocket money, went shopping the next day and came back with a tin of deep red paint, and started decorating. She only meant to paint her chair but Rose got so carried away that by the time a horrified Mum and Dad caught her, she'd also painted her chest of drawers, her table, the base of her bedside lamp, half of one wall, and – oops – quite a lot of the carpet. (Somehow I don't think it quite fitted in with our parents' idea of interior decoration. . .)

Then there was the time she got sent home from school for customizing her horrible school uniform (pity the school didn't appreciate her creativity). Not to mention the time she smuggled a stray dog into her room and kept it overnight (till Mum and Dad heard it clawing at the bedroom door in the morning, while Rose Rouge snoozed blissfully on). Or the time Rose sneaked into school early and decorated the room with a zillion homemade streamers for her favourite teacher's birthday (turning the whole day into a party for her class). And then there was that one grey, rainy day in Edinburgh when she saw a beautiful tourist poster for Balgownie – all deep purple heather hillsides and dark forests – and instead of going to school she jumped on the first bus in the bus station heading north (unfortunately, it only went as far as Perth, where Mum and Dad had to pick her up later that night).

"Omigod! That's given me a brill –"

From the high-pitched squawk she started that sentence with, Morven suddenly drops down to a barely audible whisper.

"– iant idea!"

She's staring over towards the sinks, I notice, where Jade is still washing out a plastic paint pallet, with much clattering and sploshing.

"What has?"

"What you said about Rose Rouge just then!"

"What about it?"

"Jade's birthday next week – why don't we have a surprise birthday party for her? We could hold it in the barn next to my house. I could sort out the food, with Mum's help, of course!"

Sounds great – the old barn next to the farmhouse where Morven lives is pretty gorgeous, in a picturesque, falling-down way – but I don't see what it has to do with what I've just told her about Rose Rouge.

"The zillions of homemade streamers – *you* could do those for the party!" she hissed. "You're best at art in this class – everyone knows it!"

Another compliment, another blush. But I'm pretty buzzed up on the idea.

"How would it work? Who would we invite? How could we keep it sec—"

I don't finish the sentence because there's suddenly a warm, wet sensation around my feet.

Doesn't seem that Harvey is house-trained, or make that *Portakabin*-trained quite yet. . .

11

The strange sound of scrabbling

Speaking of wee. . .

OK, so earlier today, me, Jade and Morven had a snigger or three at the idea of sleepwalkers mistaking their wardrobe for the downstairs loo. That was before tonight, before I got paranoid.

I mean, if I couldn't remember doodling round my freckles, how could I know for sure that I hadn't, well . . . y'know?!

I decided I'd better check. Which I did about half an hour ago, and I'm very pleased to report that there's nothing at the bottom of my wardrobe except a) shoes, b) a pile of magazines I might want to read again, c) some scary eyelash curlers I once chucked in there when I got bugged by not being able to figure out how to use them, and d) a whole lot of dusty fluff.

Once I'd put my mind at rest, it was time for homework.

Ahem.

Funny how my bag – packed with books – is still hanging from the back of the door, unopened since I got back from school.

And funny that my head flipped from thoughts of physics to brilliant ideas for (surprise) party decorations, just like that.

Which is why the entire floor of my bedroom is covered in a small forest's worth of paper. There are sheets and sheets of the stuff, all dragged out from under the bed, where I store it all. There are A3 sheets of card, which are mostly leftovers that Mum and Dad didn't need or use for their drawings and designs and presentations. There are sheets of plain paper in shades of lemon and lime, raspberry and chocolate, apricot and cream. There are fancy art papers, screenprinted with delicate patterns or all deliciously knobbly and textured, some of them with ghostly leaves and twigs pressed into them. There are flimsy, rustly sheets of tissue paper, that seem to puff up like poppadums when you flick through them. Then there are sheets and sheets of cool or quirky wrapping paper, that tends to end up either round people's presents (like you'd expect), cut up in collages (which you might not) or stuck on my wall (hey presto, my flock of butterflies).

I know it's a weird collection to have. But then Jenna Harris is obsessed with collecting every character in every form from *The Lion King*, and Gavin Cooper has saved every pair of trainers he's had since he was two, so maybe hoarding paper's not so weird after all. Specially since I do a lot of arty-crafty (ArTy-CrAfTy?) stuff with it.

I just wish some of the sheets had inspired me tonight. But as I shuffled and swapped them around – spreading them out across the carpet like the paper equivalent of an oil slick – no ideas for decorations stirred in my head at *all*.

Maybe that's because all that was stirring in my head was the fact that – *hello* – it was Thursday now, and I still hadn't heard from Rose Rouge. I was dying to talk to her about thunderstorms appearing out of the blue just when you're in the middle of a fairy ring, just when you're in the middle of a wish.

Since that all seemed pretty much like some sort of marshmallow magic, I decided maybe the best way to contact Rose was via marshmallow magic too. Yeah, nuts I know, but it was worth a try.

And that's why right now I'm hanging out of the

skylight with a left-over-from-Bonfire-Night sparkler in my hand.

". . .r. . .o. . .u. . .g. . .e!" I murmur, as I finish writing her name in the sunsetting sky, in a mixture of bright white twinkles and luminous orange swirls.

As the last crackling twinkle twinkles, I blow the faint plume of grey smokiness into the air, wishing my message away.

Scrabble.

The evening is full of soft sounds of birdcalls, the tumble and burble of the river and the hiss of the occasional car.

Scrabble, scrabble. Rustle, rustle, rustle, rippppp!

But *stuff* the birds and the burbling – there's a very bizarre sound coming from behind me in my room. . .

Scrabble, scrabble, rippppp!

I really don't like that scrabbling part of the noise; it's been the backing track to my nightmares the last few nights.

Scrabble.

[Silence.]

Scrabble.

[Longer silence, only interrupted by the sound of my heartbeat thundering like a pony galloping in clogs.]

Scrabble, scrabble, scrabble, scrabble. . .

I don't want to turn round and look, but I'm going to *have* to, aren't—

Eek! There's something *moving* in the tissue paper and I want to shout for Mum or Dad but there's a scream stuck in my throat and I can't move and I don't know what to do and maybe I shouldn't have done the marshmallow magic and maybe it made something bad happen and why didn't Isla protect me and where's Rose Rouge when I need her and . . . and . . . and –

Oh.

Awwww. . .

It's a mouse!

The daintiest, teensiest little house mouse.

It knows it's being gawped at by a giant (i.e. me), and it's trembling in the middle of a muddle of purple tissue paper, its impossibly weeny front paws covering its muzzle as if it's squeaking a petrified "Eek!" all of its own.

"Hi, there. . .!" I whisper, moving in slowed-down slow-motion. "Don't be scared!"

Ho ho ho. Easy for *me* to say, when I'm about a billion times bigger than this minuscule shivering thing.

But that's my problem: how do you make a wild animal the size of your thumb chill out? Smile? Hum to it? Tell it a joke to put it at its ease?

Ah, but wait . . . *I* know.

"Look, it's all right," I say super-softly, bending my knees and lowering myself floor-ward, hoping my knees or the floorboards don't creak and scare it away.

The mouse – frozen with fear and probably about to have a mini heart attack – doesn't move, doesn't blink.

"Look, I've got something for you!"

Amazingly, it stays stock-still as my hand stretches out, with the crumb of Kit-Kat I pulled out of my pocket just now.

Ooh – check it out!

There's definite sniffage going on there, a mouse nose that's only just big enough to be visible to the human eye quivering at the proximity of food. Or at least Kit-Kat. (Don't suppose any mousey nutritionists would recommend chocolate in a healthy, balanced rodent diet.)

"Come on, peanut! You can do it!" I murmur, as that itsy-bitsy whiskered nose stretches closer to my gradually advancing fingers.

Yes! I think it might just—

"Knock-knock!"

Rat-a-tat-tat.

At the speed of sound (the rustling of tissue paper), the minuscule mouse takes off, disappearing so fast that I can't even make out which part of the room it vanished to.

"Er . . . who's there?"

Thank goodness the mouse has magically evaporated; like I say, my parents aren't big fans of living things. Of the animal variety, I mean. If Mum thought there was a mouse in my room, she'd be on the 24-hour hotline to Rentokil before I could say, "But, Mum, isn't it the sweetest, little thi—"

"Boo!" she calls out, from the other side of the door.

"Um . . . boo who?"

"No need to cry!" says Mum, opening the door and grinning around it. "It's only a joke!"

Boom boom.

"Just brought you this," she tells me, nodding her head down at the tray she's carrying, with a tall tumbler of orange juice and a hunky slab of carrot cake with vanilla icing on it. "Thought you might need a bit of something to keep you going through all that homework you were moaning about having to do at teatime! Oh. . ."

The "oh" is because I plainly have no homework in front of me. Unless of course Mr Guthrie has asked us to make as much of a mess of our bedroom floors as possible. (Er. . .)

"I had an idea – for decorating Morven's barn.

For Jade's surprise party. I told you about that, right?"

"Mmm, yes. I see," says Mum, though probably all she can see is glorified litter and someone who's dodging their homework. "So did you come up with any themes?"

"Um, no."

I stare round at the floor, realizing that it's so covered in papery clutter that Mum doesn't know where to step or what to do with the tray.

"Here, let me," I tell her, tiptoeing into the tiny gaps where you can glimpse carpet and taking the tray from her. "So I was thinking, could we maybe go into Aberdeen on Saturday? Check out the art shop in Schoolhill and see if they've got anything I could use?"

"Well, Dad and I were going to work this weekend. . . But what the heck; one day won't make any difference. Yes, I'll take you there – no problem. Whatever makes you happy, Laurel!"

Now you see, if Mum'd just stopped at "no problem", it would've been fine. But no; she has to add that last "whatever makes you happy" line, which reminds me of the times in Edinburgh that she and Dad tiptoed around me, like I was as mad and mixed-up as everyone at school thought.

Rose Rouge. . .? my mind whispers, floating out

into the darkening night sky after the wisps of smoke and swirls of long-lost sparkler twirls. *Where are you?*

I need to talk to Rose. I need to know why everything feels kind of normal but at the same time *squint*. I need to know for sure what all the mad weather signs mean, what changes are coming, and how those changes will change *me*.

After all, I'm only an apprentice when it comes to marshmallow magic.

But Rose. . .

Rose Rouge can feel everything, like she's got fingertips in her mind.

Rose Rouge senses what's happening, before anyone else has even noticed a change of wind direction.

Rose Rouge reads the signs, swirling out all the possibilities in front of you.

Rose Rouge is the queen of everything.

Rose Rouge—

"Laurel!" Mum snaps, in an uncharacteristically urgent voice. "What's that smell?"

As my nostrils immediately tune in, I flip my head around and see a dancing wave of orange out of one of the skylight windows. The last traces of today's sun, melting slowly over the Glentorran mountains. . .?

Or – more accurately – the leaves in the guttering set alight by flyaway sparkler twinkles.

Help.

Forget marshmallow magic – I need a bucket of water.

Now. . .

12

Girl-shaped pancakes

"*Local Girl Puts Out Blaze With Orange Juice!*" giggles Jade.

"Or how about, *Sparkler Sparks Blaze Drama – Local Girl Arrested!*"

"*Very* funny!" I say, rolling my eyes at Jade and Morven's teasing. There was no way last night's events were going to make the front page of the weekly *Balgownie Journal* because – as Morven just pointed out – I managed to dowse the "blaze" by grabbing the glass from the tray Mum had brought up and chucking juice over the crackling leaves in the guttering.

Still, at least the bad-taste teasing was making me smile. The lecture I got from Mum and Dad last night didn't make me smile much at all. After the do-you-realize-how-dangerous-this-could-have-been? speech (yes I did and it made me feel sick), they demanded that I have a clear-out of anything flammable in my room this weekend. Which means not only the rest of the packet of sparklers, but all my pretty little tea-lights, my fairy lights (they were very cheap and don't have a safety standards mark on them), and all my paper, which Mum and Dad said they'll store for me in their plan chest in the office downstairs.

"Are you taking this seriously, Laurel?" Mum had said at one point, staring at me with worried eyes.

I'd nodded quickly, glad that she couldn't see into my mind, where there was currently an image of a tiny mouse sitting in a nest of purple tissue paper. It was bad enough that my parents had imagined their dream home reduced to charred rubble, without them thinking it was being overrun by a plague of mice too. . . .

"Did you get the dates in your diary muddled up or something, Lemmie?" says Morven now, with a wicked grin on her face.

"What are you on about?" I ask, knowing I'm being wound up but not sure how exactly.

"Did you open it in November, instead of June? Did you get the sparklers out because you thought it was Bonfire Night?"

"Look, enough with the jokes!" I say, arching my eyebrows mock-sternly first at Jade and then at Morven. "We're wasting time! We've got Pooh sticks to play!"

We're fooling around on the Braeden Bridge, the hundred-year-old granite arch that stretches across the river. Me, Morven and Jade are celebrating finishing school for the week by playing a game of Pooh sticks with whatever comes to hand (i.e. not sticks). I've got a wilting daisy chain, Morven has a scrunchie that's lost its elastic and Jade has nothing, *yet*.

"Come on, Jade!" I say, deliberating nudging her arm as she rummages in her bag. "There's got to be *something* in there that you don't mind dumping!"

"Well, not really! I don't carry tons of junk around with me, like you two!"

"Hey, you're not chucking *that* in the water, are you?" Morven suddenly asks Jade, stunned to see her pulling out a shiny new magazine that she only just bought as we walked along here.

"No, but I don't think I'm going to miss this shampoo ad on the back page much, do you?"

After a swift tear, Jade stuffs the rest of the mag back in her bag and dumps it at her feet. Then with a deft fold, tuck and bend, she has herself a paper airplane, all ready to make its maiden flight – destination: the tumbling water below.

"OK . . . everyone ready?" I say, as we all lean our arms on the thick, stony parapet.

"Yep!"

"Uh-huh!"

"Then . . . one, two, twelve, GO!!!"

As soon as the daisy chain, scrunchie and paper plane sail from our hands, we all swivel around, ready to dash across to the other side of the bridge to see whose lookalike Pooh stick comes first – and almost get splatted into girl-flavoured pancakes by a convoy of speeding lorries.

The slipstream of air as they hurtle by whips the breath out of my lungs and slaps my hair round my face, blinding me for a second. All I can think of is that I must be some sort of jinx – last night, I nearly burnt the house down and now I've had a near-squashed experience.

"Wow. . ." mumbles Morven, sweeping her own tangled hair back into place.

"*That* was close."

As Jade speaks, she shakes her shiny dark hair back on to her shoulders, her deep brown eyes following the rattling lorries as they rumble into town.

"Look – they've got the name of a construction company on their sides," she points out. "They must be on their way to Craigandarroch!"

"Can we see the Lodge from here?" I ask in a

panic, scanning the road before hurrying across to the other side.

It's a stupid question that I already know the answer to (and the answer is nope). But it doesn't stop me standing on my tiptoes, staring off at the densely wooded hill at the other side of town, over the rooftops, past the church spires. I don't know what I expect to see: half the trees as flattened as me and my friends nearly were just now? Or a giant placard on the hillside spelling out "SAVE OUR LODGE!" hung there by dedicated protesters?

Actually, I think *I'm* the only person in the village who isn't happy about the Lodge going – everyone else seems delighted at the idea of the spa resort opening and the chance for more jobs in the area. Morven's parents are hoping the people in charge will be looking for local produce for their kitchens, while Jade's grandparents are keeping their fingers crossed that lots of the spa's guests will want to sneak away from the strictly healthy menu they'll be getting served and come for a full-on, five-course Chinese meal at the Jade Palace instead.

I might not like it, but I do get why the whole of Balgownie's so keen on the new resort. What I *don't* get is why they don't seem sad to see something so beautiful and neglected as the Lodge crushed into nothingness.

"Lemmie! Jade! Take a look at that!" Morven says suddenly, pointing down towards the river.

I drop my gaze, and see it.

A young stag – on the river's edge nearest town – stepping gingerly down the uneven, rocky bank, his delicate, rangy front legs already out of sight in the swirling, surging water.

In another few seconds, he's right in the thick of the heady flow downstream, fighting not to be caught by it. His neck is held stiff, his antlers held high, his expression determined but terrified, as he focuses on the opposite bank.

"What's it doing?" asks Jade, transfixed at the sight of the young stag's struggles.

"He doesn't look very old. He's probably been forced out of the herd he's grown up in by the dominant stag. I bet he's just heading out to try and find his own territory," says Morven.

You can sometimes catch Morven moaning about being brought up in a small town, so far away from cities and civilization (i.e. big shopping centres with handy branches of TopShop etc.). But right now I'm suddenly, properly jealous of her being such a country girl, rooted to the trees and the hills and the history of the area, through the grandparents and great-grandparents and great-great-grandparents times ten that came before her.

"I just thought that deer was a bit hot, and maybe fancied a swim," mumbles Jade, showing that she might score forty-eight out of fifty in a French test but knows precisely nothing about the life of wildlife.

Not that I'm much better; I wouldn't be able to explain why exactly that young stag is willing to do something so wild, something so risky. All I know – as I watch him breathlessly scrambling for a foothold as he reaches the other bank – is that it's a sign. It's *more* than a sign; it's a powerful rush in my stomach. I want, just for a second, to feel as wild and reckless as that stag. . .

"He's made it!" Jade laughs breathlessly, like she's forgotten to inhale air in the last few seconds.

She's right – the stag is bounding up the bank, across the main road and up into the pine-covered forest. There's a final faint sliver of silver-brown hide visible as he darts off between the trees.

"Lemmie! What are you *doing*?!" shrieks Morven.

"It's OK," I giggle, holding my hands out to keep my balance as I wobble myself upright on the bridge parapet.

"Lem! *Please* get down! You could fall!"

"It's all right!" I tell Jade, though I avoid looking down at her in case it makes me go wibbly and lose my balance. "It's great up here – I can see much further. I can see the top of Craigandarroch Lodge and . . . and. . ."

And the crane that's erected beside it, the one that's there, presumably, to knock the Lodge down.

For a second, I do go wibbly, making Morven and Jade shriek some more, before I tilt and wobble myself into a steady position again.

"Hey . . . Lemmie. . .!" a distant boy's voice calls out. "Planning on going for a swim?!"

"It's just Jack McLennan – don't pay any attention – just come down!" Jade urges me.

But I can see better than she can that it's Jack doing the shouting; he's just come out of a turning beside the potter's gallery with Kyle and Iain. Kyle's grinning at me again. He either thinks I'm incredibly brave or (gulp) incredibly insane, I don't know which. Though I know which I'd prefer. . .

"Oooooof!"

I'm still trying to interpret Kyle's smile when I feel each arm being grabbed hard, and I tumble out of (nearly) thin air on to hard tarmac.

"What are you doing?"

"Yeah, what were you trying to prove?"

My friends' panicked voices babble together and I can't make out who asked what.

"Look, I just felt like –"

But my explanations stop as a shutter comes down

on what I'm saying, just as that dark cupboard door is thrown open in my head.

Which is the exact same time as I get down from the parapet.

Which is the exact same time as I see the silver car drive slowly past us.

Which is the exact same time as that girl in the back seat stares directly into my eyes.

Which is the exact same time as I know for sure that it's definitely the wicked witch of my bad dreams, and not just some pretty teenage holidaymaker in town who happens to look like her.

Which is the exact same time every single thing that Sian Ellis ever did to make my life *hell* comes shooting into pin-sharp focus.

And that dark cupboard in my head? I think some of those dusty secrets of mine might just come tumbling out. . .

13

Gold star for bullying

Y'know, I feel sorry for anyone who's been kicked, punched, or tripped up by a bully.

It's never happened to me.

I've watched programmes on telly and stories in books about people who've been forced to hand over lunch money, or mobiles or whatever to bullies.

That's never happened to me either.

What happened to me at primary school was . . . Sian Ellis.

"I'll just have a Coke," I half-shout at Mhairi the waitress, who happens to be Shonagh Robertson's big sister. (It's a small town – everyone just about knows everyone.)

I'm half-shouting because of the noise in the Balgownie café this Friday afternoon. The old-fashioned caff is pretty big, spreading across what used to be two shops way back whenever, but today it's mobbed with schoolkids, piles of mums with pushchairs, and a group of American tourists. Every table of schoolkids is talking at roaring volume, a couple of babies are screaming, the American tourists are asking each other very loudly what stuff on the menu means ("Say, what are 'tatties and neeps'?!"), and the radio is blaring out the latest chart music (at the height of summer, this gets changed to a never-ending tape of corny Scottish folk music for the holidaymakers).

Me, Jade and Morven were lucky to get a table. Or maybe we're not – it is the tiny one right beside the gents' toilets.

"And I'll have an orange juice, please," Jade tells Mhairi.

"Yeah, I'll have an orange juice as well, thanks. With lots of ice. And can you bring her some apple pie and ice cream too?"

Morven's pointing at me when she says that. I try and splutter after Mhairi that I don't want the pudding that Morven's forcing on me for some reason, but she's already off to translate the menu for the Americans.

"Look, you need to eat, Lemmie," says Morven, explaining herself. "Maybe you felt dizzy on the bridge 'cause you didn't have enough for lunch."

She sounds very like her mum when she says that. Mrs McGregor thinks anyone who eats less than four meals a day (plus several snacks) is on the verge of anorexia.

"Maybe," I shrug, happier for at least one of my friends to believe I was woozy from lack of apple pie back on the bridge than traumatized by the sight of Sian Ellis. Who saw me, just the same as I saw her. Maybe it was just as much of a shock for Sian – after all, she didn't know we'd moved here. Mum and Dad started house-hunting during the summer holidays last year. When Sian last saw (I mean, *blanked* me), as far as *she* knew, we'd be turning up at the same secondary school in a few weeks' time, ready for a whole new level of bullying. But I spoiled her fun by moving away. . .

Jade is staring at me, in that staring way she does so well. She doesn't buy that lack-of-food-wooziness thing; she's dragged me here for a bit of an interrogation.

"So the girl in the car – she was *definitely* the girl you thought you recognized before, right, Lemmie? The one you saw in the street on Monday?"

Definitely. Sadly.

"Yeah . . . her name's Sian," I say.

"So she must be in Balgownie on holiday, if Jade

saw her at the rented cottage across the road from hers."

As she talks, Morven fans herself with a laminated menu.

"Mmm, must be," I mumble in reply.

"And you said you weren't very friendly with her at your old school?" says Jade.

MY ANSWER: "Like I said, she always thought she was kind of 'it', if you see what I mean."

THE TRUTH: Sian Ellis was a witch. Or at least a bully, which was just as bad. My own, personal bully. She was "it" all right; smart and pretty and popular. She had so much going for her she didn't need to be a bully at all, but did it for pure fun anyway. Bullying me was her hobby, and could've become her full-time job she was so dedicated and good at it. She could've won a gold star or *prizes* even for her exceptional bullying skills, if anyone but me knew about them, of course. But that was part of Sian's amazing talent; slipping all those mean and sarcastic barbs my way while everyone else got her sugar-coated smiles and chatty charm. . .

"So you and your mates didn't like her much?" asks Morven, getting straight to the point, while she frantically fan-fans.

MY ANSWER: "Nah, not much, I suppose."

THE TRUTH: Sammi, Carys and Nicola *adored*

Sian, at least once she flattered them into being friends with her. I guess when Sian started at school, she looked around for potential buddies and my three mates fitted the bill. . . In their own ways, Sammi (Greek and gorgeous), Carys (cute blonde) and Nicola (couldn't be cooler) were as pretty and perfect as Sian Ellis. And in *my* own way, I was the joker of our gang, the one who fooled around, the one who got teased by the others for her dumb dress sense. But Sian only wanted a posse of princesses, and I was no longer required. It took her a long time and a lot of work, but bit by subtle bit, she turned my friends against me, as well as everyone in my class – including my teacher.

"Guess you won't be knocking on her cottage door, offering to show her around town, then?" smiles Jade, just as Mhairi comes back with our order, and slams drinks and apple pie 'n' ice cream down on the table.

MY ANSWER: "I don't *think* so!"

THE TRUTH: I feel totally *ill* just knowing Sian Ellis is in town, walking the same pavements as me, breathing the same pine-scented air I do, leaving a trail of venom drifting behind her wherever she goes. . .

"Thing is, Lemmie," says Morven, crunching on an ice-cube from her glass, "it's Friday now, and you first spotted that Sian girl on Monday. Holiday lets work Saturday to Saturday, so she could be gone by tomorrow anyway!"

Yesss! I cheer silently to myself.

"Unless her family's here for a fortnight's holiday, of course," Jade adds.

Nooo! I groan silently to myself – as a hand darts in front of my face, and a finger scoops a dollop of ice cream straight off my apple pie.

I glance up and see first a skinny body, then a Phat Farm T-shirt, and then Kyle Strachan's grinning face, as he sticks his ice-cream flavoured finger in his mouth.

"Mmmm, not bad!" he says, as he shuffles casually backwards towards the door, with Iain and Jack mooching and grinning alongside him as usual.

OK.

I reckon I have exactly two seconds to say something back to him – hopefully something funny and/or cool – before he's out of that door.

One. . .

I've just got a stupid smile on my face.

Two. . .

And my mind's gone blank.

Gone. . .

"Wow, he *so* likes you!" says Morven, practically leaning herself right across the table towards me in her excitement.

"No *way* – he's just winding me up," I tell her, with a dismissive, embarrassed shake of the head.

(Though I'm not sure if I *completely* believe that.)

"Lemmie, if Kyle wasn't just flirting with you, then I'm an ostrich," states Jade, matter-of-factly.

Jade's a smart girl, and she certainly isn't an ostrich, as far as I can see.

Maybe I should do like Rose Rouge told me to, and think of the shiny stuff. Like, *yeah*, so my old enemy is in Balgownie; but she could be gone tomorrow, fingers crossed.

And the most gorgeous boy in my year might just have been flirting with me, which is a much, *much* shinier thing to concentrate on. . .

14

Good riddance . . . I *wish*

"Penny for your thoughts, Laurel!" says Mum, flipping her shiny wine-coloured hair my way as she steals a quick look at me before gazing back at the road.

In front of us is the sign that says, "Welcome to Balgownie". An hour's drive behind us is Aberdeen, where we've just been.

Mum and Dad: they might try and act strict sometimes, but I know they're really tough as custard, with squirty cream on top. 'Cause whatever they said on Thursday night during their lecture, they seem to have forgotten it all. At least Mum never mentioned a thing about clearing out my room the whole day we spent in Aberdeen together. She just seemed to want to have fun, like trying on old lady hats in Debenhams and making us stop to eat tea and cake every half hour. Besides that, she's been happy to pay for gallons more stuff to clutter up my room. I still haven't decided what style decorations to do for Jade's party next week, but that hasn't stopped me buying a bunch of on-offer sheets of ice-cream coloured paper. And the stuff out of the Pound shop in the Market Hall was just feel-good tat for me: a snow dome ornament with a space for a photo to slip inside it; a fruitbowl of life-size plastic fruit and a tiny bamboo box that I hadn't a clue what I'd do with.

"Um. . ." I say, wriggling about in my seat trying to think of how to answer Mum's question without giving away what had been fugging up my mind for the last twenty minutes. "Just daydreaming, really."

"Daydreaming about anything nice?"

Daydreaming that Sian Ellis and her parents have already packed up their suitcases and checked out of their holiday cottage, hopefully. I've spent the last hour on the main road scanning for silver cars heading away (far, *far* away) from Balgownie.

But I'm not about to tell Mum that. Or Dad.

Well, they didn't exactly take the threat of Sian very seriously in Edinburgh; they let my teacher Mrs O'Farrell convince them that any "problems" I had couldn't *possibly* have anything to do with the wonderful, the angelic Sian Ellis, no matter what *I* said. So why would they take it seriously now? (By the way, I might have resented Mum and Dad for that back then, but since we moved to Balgownie I've tried – *hard* – to wipe the slate clean, if you know what I mean. A new town, a new life, a new start...)

"Here we are!" says Mum cheerfully, turning the car into our narrow street, then whacking on the handbrake as she parks outside our house.

"Hi, girls!"

That's Dad; he must have seen us pull up.

"Wow – bought out the craft shop as usual, Laurel?" he laughs, opening the boot to help us with our shopping. "And what's this – a hat?"

"Put it down!" I tell him, making a grab for the bowl of plastic fruit he's trying to balance on his head.

"And what's this – it's a swizz! There's nothing inside but a blizzard!" he says, putting the fruit bowl down but now shaking a shower of snowflakes in my snow dome.

"There's a slot *there* – you fit a photo of someone in it."

"Mmmm!" Dad nods. "To think someone gets paid to sit in a design studio and come up with useless stuff like this!! *Ow!* No! I'm sorry for teasing, Laurel! *Ow!*"

Being hit by plastic fruit doesn't really hurt, but

Dad pretends it does, as he ducks back into the house with bags of shopping, and pineapples, oranges and bananas bouncing off his head.

We're all still laughing as we close the front door and pile the bags messily in the pristine hall, when Dad suddenly goes and blows it.

"Hey, Chrissie, got a call when you guys were out," Dad turns and says to Mum. "The new project manager for the spa resort – he says the tender is going out for the interior design of the bar area. He's asked us to get our ideas in soon!"

So Mum and Dad are the same as everyone else in the town: happy to see the Lodge flattened if it means they can make some money. It feels like they're traitors somehow.

"Oh, that's great, Mike! It would really make our name if we could do something public like that, instead of just people's houses!"

"And that's not all . . . and this'll interest you too, Laurel. Guess who the project manager is?"

"Who?" Mum shrugs.

"Rory Ellis!"

Mum's face freezes in a smile. Much like the blood in my veins does. I don't know the name Rory, but the name Ellis is horribly familiar. *Please* say it's not her dad, *please* say it's not her dad, *please* say it's not—

"*You* know," Dad continues brightly to my mum. "Rory Ellis – we got chatting to him one parents' night at Laurel's old school. He's the dad of that girl in Laurel's class. That girl Sia –"

Now it's Dad's turn to freeze, as a) he remembers the whole me-blaming-Sian-for-my-problems/Mum-and-him-not-choosing-to-believe-me thing, and b) he confirms my worst suspicions. This Rory Ellis bloke is Sian Ellis's dad. He is the father of the wicked witch. Omigod.

"Let's get these bags of groceries through to the kitchen!" Mum suddenly announces, widening her eyes meaningfully at Dad, like I'm too dippy or dumb to notice.

"Um . . . right. . ." mumbles Dad, picking up far too many weighted-down supermarket carrier bags at the same time in his haste to follow Mum's orders. "Yes. Of course. We can talk about all that, um, boring business stuff later. . ."

I drift off and out of Mum and Dad's conversation. Rolls of paper under one arm, bag of tat in one hand, I take the stairs two at a time.

Feeling too frazzled to even notice I'm doing it, I kiss the tip of my finger and press it against Isla's soft cloth face and throw the door of my room open.

"Where have you been? I've been waiting for ages!"

Rose Rouge is stretched out on my bed, leaning against a mass of cushions, flicking through a magazine. She's wearing a skirt made of black netting with uneven edges, like it's some kind of ballet costume that got chewed up by a psycho tumble-dryer. On top, she's got on a tie-dye T-shirt in shades of pink, red and mauve, with an image of a big pair of cherries right on the front. She's got some new purple and red twists in her hair too. Even though it's warm outside, she's still wearing her flowery Doc Martens, with one pink sock and one red sock peeking out of the top of each boot. Some people (i.e. those with an imagination bypass) might think she looks ridiculous, but I think she just looks ridiculously amazing.

"Oh! I didn't expect . . . I mean, I didn't know you were here!" I waffle in surprise.

That's dumb of me to say.

Why *shouldn't* Rose Rouge be here? Hadn't I sent plenty of SOS messages, by phone and by marshmallow magic?

"You should've let me know you were coming – I would've got Mum to bring us back earlier!"

"What, and spoil the surprise?!" she smiles back at me, stretching her arms up above her tinkling tendrils of hair. "I like your little friend, by the way."

It takes me a second to figure out who she's on

about, till I spot the tiny grey shape on the plate by my bedside. Watching me with worried beady eyes, the mouse carries on frantically nibbling at the cracker crumbs it's stumbled upon, trying to get as many crammed in its mouth before any giants shoo it away.

"Hey!" says Rose, slapping her hands together and sending my new friend scurrying for cover. "Fancy going for a walk, peanut?"

I'm actually more in the mood to run far, far away, but I'll settle for a walk – especially if it's with Rose Rouge.

"I can't believe it!" Rose gasps.

Me and Rose Rouge, we're standing at the winding footpath that leads into Craigandarroch woods. The only problem is, we can't get to it – the whole perimeter of the woods is ringed off and made out of bounds by a towering metal bracelet of fencing.

"It's like being told that you can't do what you want to do any more," says Rose Rouge, tossing her waist-length dreads behind her angrily, and kicking a section of fencing with the toe of her prettily patterned Doc Marten boot. "It's like being *bullied*."

She's just mentioned the "B" word. I guess it's a good time to mention the "S" word. The only person who knows everything about what happened with Sian is Rose Rouge. The only one who totally believed *my* side of the story back then was Rose Rouge. I wanted to wait till we were here, till we were in (or at least near) our special, favourite place – and, *well* out of Mum and Dad's hearing – to blurt out the whole saga.

"Rose?" I begin, a funny little wobble edging into my voice. "I saw—"

An electronic, bird-like bleep interrupts my soul-baring session. Distractedly, Rose Rouge slips her hand into her patchwork bag and pulls out her mobile.

"Oh, no . . . not *already*!" she mutters, checking her text. "Listen, I've got to go, peanut!"

The sun's beating down on us, but I feel a shiver of a chill.

"Go where? You just got here!" I say to her, confused.

"Sorry, Lem – there's a party. Someone at art school . . . it's at their gran's holiday cottage, or their aunt's or whoever's. It's near here. Near-ish, anyway. Everyone's on their way up. Someone's coming to meet me in the Square – I just didn't expect them to be here so soon!"

"But I thought you'd come to see *me*!?" I say, knowing I sound like a weedy five year old who's not getting a trip to Legoland.

"Well, I did! *Sort* of. . ." Rose Rouge says, wincing with awkwardness. "On my way to the party . . . that's what I thought!"

And *I* thought (OK, *hoped*) Rose Rouge wasn't going to fade away from me.

Now I'm not so sure that I can *be* that sure.

Right, I think, as I watch Rose Rouge blow me a kiss, then hurry off down the road into town and towards the bridge. *So this week*:

1) I've found out that my favourite place is going to get bulldozed.

2) My parents have banged on again about ripping my lovely room to bits and rebuilding it.

3) I nearly set fire to the house.

4) I nearly got squashed by a fleet of lorries.

5) I've been let down by Rose Rouge.

6) I've been let down by the marshmallow magic.

7) Sian Ellis is flapping her evil bat wings around town.

If that weird weather last weekend was a sign that something was going to change, then I think it's happening.

And what's changing is my luck, from glitteringly good to really, truly *rotten*. . .

15

Well, hel-luau, hel-luau

"Where's Morv?" says Jade impatiently, standing on her tiptoes to try and see past the throng streaming into the assembly hall this Monday morning. "Can you see her?"

It's pretty funny; even though she's on her tiptoes, Jade is so small she doesn't even stretch to the level of other people's shoulders.

But I'm not laughing at her. She's too good a friend for that. When I called her from my room on Saturday night – with Rose Rouge long gone and no one but a mouse and a door angel to talk to – she helped me scrabble some hope back, just when I needed it most.

"Er, here's some gossip for you. You know that girl from my old school I don't like much?" I'd said to her, trying to sound less stressed then I really was. "My dad mentioned that *her* dad is going to be working at the new resort development for the next year."

"So?" Jade had said in her usual, reassuringly matter-of-fact way. "Are you thinking that she's going to be here for a year too?"

"Um, I guess so," I replied, trying to sound like the idea had only just occurred to me.

"Well, I doubt it. I mean, if they have a house in Edinburgh, the whole family aren't going leave it sitting empty for a year and move up here, taking their daughter out of school and everything, are they?"

"Aren't they?"

"Look, Lemmie – they've been staying at a holiday cottage, right? I bet that Sian and her mum have just been up visiting her dad. After this, he'll probably be staying in a flat in Balgownie during the week, and heading back home to Edinburgh at the weekend."

I'd hoped Jade didn't hear my huge sigh of relief. Even though she didn't know it, she'd told me the best thing I could have heard. There was no one I trusted more than Jade to be logical and calm. With a couple of sensible sentences, she'd helped me feel a little flicker of shininess again.

Later, I'd managed to drift off to sleep OK, till I suddenly woke up on my knees in a circle of moonlight on the bedroom carpet, with a red felt pen poised *just* above a freckle. I'd gasped, feeling kind of breathless and disorientated, till my eyes came to rest on a glowing bundle of blue-ness dangling from the dressing table mirror . . . it was my lei, my beautiful, 100% plastic lei. And that's when a sparkle of inspiration twinkled into the fuzz of my mind: Jade's party. It could be a luau! Which is of course a Hawai—

"Hey, hi, Lemmie!"

The sandy hair, the sunny smile, the sheer gorgeousness of Kyle Strachan.

Helppppp. . .

I want to nudge Jade, but she's vanished; disappeared into the pressing, pushing surge while I had a head full of Hawaiian flowers for a second there. I clench my hands in a panic but that just makes me wince: I have the tender fingertips of someone who sat and made fifty paper garlands and a stupid amount of flowery decorations all day yesterday. . .

"I, um, like your T-shirt!" says Kyle, grinning at me.

Helppppp. . .

This seems to be almost like the start of a proper conversation. I'm probably as red as the cherries on the front of my top.

"Yeah?" I manage to say, sounding (I hope) almost normal.

It's on the tip of my tongue to say that Rose Rouge lent me the T-shirt – not that Kyle will have a clue who Rose Rouge is – but then he dives right back in.

"Um, I was talking to Morven just now," he nods over his shoulder, in the vague direction of wherever he might have seen my missing-in-action friend.

"Yeah?"

"Uh-huh. She told me about Jade's party on Saturday. How it's a secret and everything."

"Yeah. . ."

Oh, *please* let me stop being so tongue-knottingly nervous. Please let me say something apart from "yeah".

"She said it's got a kind of tropical theme thing."

Kyle looks like he's very chilled out when he's talking, but then I can't help noticing he's got his hands bunched into nervous fists in his baggy skater trousers. That should make me feel better, but it doesn't.

"Um . . . yeah," I nod at him, not even able to tell him it's not tropical; it's Hawaiian. A proper Hawaiian luau (i.e. celebration) with leis for every guest as they arrive. And Hawaiian food, if Morven and her mum can find any recipes on the net.

"I was. . ." Kyle shrugs. "I was *just* sort of wondering if you'd give me your mobile number, Lemmie."

What!

Today's feather (a cuckoo's) is in the pocket of my red denim skirt. Right now it's getting squeezed into a twisted, wispy blob in my fingers.

"I . . . uh . . . just thought it would be a good idea. 'Cause of the party being secret, I thought I could maybe call you on Saturday morning or something, to check it was, uh, all still on."

Kyle's banoffee skin is tinged with pink. Omigod, I've made the coolest boy I know blush, without even trying.

"Um . . . yeah!"

(Come on, Lemmie! You can do better than that!)

"Here, I've got a pen," I mumble, fumbling in my bag. "If you want me to write it down for you, I mean. If you want."

(OK, so that was a bit waffly, but it was definitely an improvement on "yeah".)

"Now then, people! Can we all be seated! Quick as you can, please!"

That's Mr Murray, the head, barking out orders from the podium. I have exactly ten seconds while everyone scuffles and settles to do one of two things: look around and find Morven and/or Jade, or scribble my mobile number down on the scrap of paper for Kyle. Guess which I choose?

"Ta!" says Kyle, his hazel eyes twinkling at me as he

takes the bit of paper and plonks down on the nearest seat. Speedily, before Mr Murray can zone in on me, I scan around and see there's a seat free at the end of the aisle, two rows back from Kyle.

Which means I have a perfect, uninterrupted view of the back of his head while Mr Murray drones on about the parents' night this week, and whatever else headteachers happen to think is important (i.e. stuff nobody else is remotely interested in).

Who'd've believed it? Kyle Strachan, asking for my number. Even if he was pretending it was something to do with the party, it still means one very important thing: KYLE STRACHAN HAS MY PHONE NUMBER!

Maybe he'll phone me sometime! Maybe just for a chat, or maybe (gulp) to ask (it's too much to hope for!) me out (faint, *thud*. . .).

"Now before we all get off to lessons," Mr Murray burbles on in the background of my daydreams, "I want to welcome a new face to the school."

No.

"It's a difficult time to join a new school, at the tail end of a term, but I hope you'll all look out for –"

Please, no.

"– Sian Ellis, who'll be in class Y1B."

No, no, *no*!

"So can you stand up, wherever you are, Sian?

Splendid. And can we all give Sian a round of applause to make her feel at home?"

I slink further down in my hard wooden chair, as Sian Ellis stands up and gives a confident smile and wave back at the thunderclaps of hands around the hall.

Which don't include mine, if you hadn't guessed. My paper-cut hands are stubbornly silent, staying clenched together on my lap. Only now they've suddenly slapped themselves over my mouth, as my stomach starts to heave.

Mr Murray has just dismissed everyone; there's the usual kerfuffle of voices and screeching chairs going on all around me.

Please don't let me be sick.

"Hey, you gonna move or what?" says the fifth-year boy I happen to have sat down next to.

"Uh, sorry. I – I –"

Oh, God. . .

"Lemmie. . .?"

I can just make out Kyle's anxious voice as I dive past him and push my way through the shuffling crowds before I barf in front of the *whole* of Balgownie Academy.

Oh, yes. People can be allergic to all sorts of stuff, like nuts, milk, eggs, seafood or whatever.

Can I help it if I'm allergic to Sian Ellis. . .?

16

Whispered shouting

Q. What do you, me, Madonna, Prince Charles, your local postman, the president of Bulgaria and everyone in the cosmiverse have in common?

A: Bladders.

Yep, it doesn't matter how posh or poor you are, or whether you're a celebrity or plain sane and normal, you still need to pee. And bladders are annoying, aren't they? They don't care if you're really busy, or far away from a loo – when they're full they don't let you forget about it.

Right now, I feel miserable and still a bit sick, and all I want to do is crawl under the duvet and hibernate till I feel better – or till Sian Ellis's year in Balgownie is up, preferably – but, oh no, my bladder has other ideas.

So now I'll have to stomp downstairs to the bathroom before I can sink into my mattress-shaped pit of gloom.

Then again. . . .

I'm on the second-from-the-top step, and a certain sound makes me stop in my tracks: the sound of whispered shouting.

It's the way my mum and dad like to argue. I guess it would be horrible if you had the sort of parents who screamed and yelled and chucked mugs and stuff at each other when they were fighting, but there's something unsettling about whispered shouting too. Maybe it's 'cause it's done at such a low volume that you can't actually make out what's being argued about, but the sharp, biting hiss of the words still sends icy spikes of dread into your heart.

What are they talking about?

I take another couple of steps down and try and hold my breath, so I can hear better.

"Well, it's not much help, you saying, 'Don't worry', is it? Because of *course* I'm going to worry!"

It's working – I can hear more; more of Mum fretting. I concentrate on standing even stiller, as if that helps me hear better too.

"But Chrissie—"

"Look, I've got to take this up to her," Mum is saying brusquely, cutting off Dad's sentence.

Uh-oh. It suddenly dawns on me that I can hear Mum more clearly not because I'm listening better but because she's getting *nearer*. . . I don't want to get caught earwigging, so I turn and fast-forward myself back up the stairs, closing the bedroom door silently and speedily behind me.

It's only when I'm huddled under the duvet that I realize my heart is thundering like someone's playing a pair of castanets in my chest and my bladder's yelling "Got to go NOW!" Tough – it'll just have to wait.

"Knock-knock. . ."

Tappity-tap.

"Who's there?" I mumble, without much enthusiasm, from under the duvet.

I don't know if Mum can hear me properly, but she must have heard enough of a "mumf-mumf?" to know that I was responding to her.

"A little old lady!"

"A little old lady who?" (or "Mumf-mumfy-mumf-mumfy-mumf?")

"Hey, I didn't know you could yodel!"

As Mum delivers the punchline, her voice gets louder so I know she's in the room. I don't feel like coming out of my padded cocoon – even though it's boiling under here – so it takes Mum to lift the corner of the duvet before we can make eye contact.

"Did you like my joke?" she asks, kneeling down and smiling in at me.

It was pretty funny. Any other time – when I wasn't feeling lousy – I might have even giggled.

"It's new," I say, gazing at my mum sideways, my pounding head squashed into the pillow.

"I looked it up on the internet just now. Thought you deserved a brand new knock-knock joke since you were sick."

"Thanks."

I want to smile, but my mouth's on strike.

"Are you feeling better now you're lying down?"

"A bit."

"I phoned the school secretary and explained that you have some kind of bug."

"Mmm," I mumble, blinking out of the cocoon at Mum.

"Maybe it's something going around," says Mum, slipping her hand under the duvet and placing it on my forehead. It feels cool and wonderful.

"Well, listen, I've left you a cold drink here, Laurel. Just try and sleep. If you need anything, shout – we'll be down in the office working on sketches today."

"Thanks."

Mum looks a bit frazzled, I notice – her normally neat hair's sort of ruffled like she's been running her hands through it. I know the second she passes a mirror and catches sight of her reflection she'll be tut-tutting and reaching for a comb, but I actually kind of like it mussed up like that. It makes her look more like she does in the old photos of her and dad when they were students together at art school.

I wonder what made her start with the hair ruffling, and whispered shouting for that matter? Is it 'cause of the tight deadline she and Dad have got to submit a design to the spa people? Or is it the fact that I came home from school feeling ill?

"Well, I'll leave you to rest. . ."

And then her hand is gone and it's dark inside the duvet and I can hear her loafers pad-padding softly down the stairs.

Once I'm sure she's safely downstairs, I throw back the duvet and stare blankly around my room, at the mounds of decorations draped on top of the dressing table and piled on the floor. Mum's pulled the blinds on the skylight windows down, but the sun is still squeezing through the slithers of gaps round the edges.

It's light enough to see the tiny mouse emerging from the pile of decorations in the corner.

"Hi!" I whisper softly.

It stops, looking like it's holding its breath, same as I did on the stairs a couple of minutes ago.

"Surprised to see me? Bet you expected to get the place to yourself today!"

Whiskers twizzle, front paws rub worriedly together.

"I'm not well," I explain to it. "I've got Sian-itis. It's a bad allergic reaction to witches."

The mouse seems to be feeling a bit braver; it zippetty-zips its way a little closer then stops to stare at me again. Its tiny dark, dotted eyes stare up at me, like it's trying to work out what I am. Course what I am is just a big bundle of nerves, shaped like a girl.

"What? Why haven't I told Mum and Dad that Sian's the problem?" I whisper in answer to a question the mouse hasn't actually asked (I *am* demented, it's true). "Because I tried before and they didn't believe me. They believed my teacher instead of me, and my teacher believed *Sian* instead of me. No one believed me. Except Rose Rouge."

I'm making it sound simple, but it wasn't – it was hard and it was horrible and it lasted three whole years. Maybe it's time for a step-by-step guide to that whole, general horribleness. . .

STEP ONE: Sian steals all my friends from me. Sammi's mum once said I was "a real individual", but Sian manages to convince everyone that I'm not an "individual", I'm a weirdo. I tell my parents; they make sympathetic noises and mutter stuff about how friendships do change, and then go back to their work.

STEP TWO: The more my old friends turn away from me, the harder I try to impress them. But the more cartwheels and kooky stuff I do, the more they think Sian is right, and I'm a weirdo. I tell my parents; they say I'm brilliant and should just ignore people ignoring me at school (hard, since that's *everyone*) and then go back to their work.

STEP THREE: The more I feel frozen out, the more Sian enjoys it, and starts putting the knife in. I tell my parents; they seem to take me seriously. They talk to Mrs O'Farrell; she says she'll investigate and get back to them. When she does, she reassures them categorically, absolutely, cross-her-heart-and-hope-to-die that *no* bullying is going on. Sian Ellis had burst into tears when she'd asked her about it, she tells them. And star pupil, golden girl Sian had suggested that perhaps I was *jealous* of her. Mrs O'Farrell asks if the problem doesn't lie at home, since it's true that my erratic, attention-seeking behaviour is a concern.

STEP FOUR: Sian, acting hurt, tells everyone I've been accusing her of bullying. Everyone likes me even *less*, if that's possible.

STEP FIVE: I run away.

STEP SIX: The school (i.e. Mrs O'Farrell) suggests

to my parents that I see a child psychologist. I see him three times, and talk to him about stuff I like to do (handstands), what my favourite subjects at school are (art, English) and why I ran away (I lie and tell him I was bored). I don't tell him about the bullying, since there's no point trying to get anyone to believe me – it hasn't done me any good so far. The psychologist tells my parents that I'm fine – a little highly strung, maybe, but smart and sane and certainly not in need of any more appointments with him.

STEP SEVEN: Sian Ellis sees a note on Mrs O'Farrell's desk, excusing me from class to go to one of my appointments with the psychologist. She sends the news round in Chinese whispers. Now I'm a proper, certified weirdo, loony, freak, whatever. No one in class speaks to me, except for this one time in the playground when they all gather round me and start chanting and shouting. Cue recurring nightmares.

"You know something?" I whisper to the mouse. "During that whole time, if I hadn't had Rose Rouge to talk to – or the marshmallow magic – I'd have gone as mad as everyone seemed to want me to be. . ."

The mouse – who's been sitting so still it's been looking more like a statue of a mouse – suddenly seems to remember something very, very urgent it's got to do, and skedaddles in a beige-grey blur.

Which reminds me of something urgent too.

'Cause even when your life's instantly gone from rainbow-tinted to rubbish, a girl's still got to do what a girl's got to do. I realize that as I tiptoe down the stairs towards the bathroom and curse my unsympathetic bladder. . .

17

Armed and loaded with charms

Last night I gave myself homework: marshmallow magic homework. It's just that I knew if I was going to make it to school today, I was going to need a *lot* of help.

With the small mouse popping out to watch me from time to inquisitive time, I lit a circle of tea-lights (not yet confiscated by Mum and Dad) on the dressing table. Next, I placed my chunk of rose quartz crystal in the middle (rose quartz: good for calming and protecting).

OK, once the rose quartz was all set – getting on with its calming and protecting – it was time to do the Star-Singing thing.

Star-Singing: it's a really strong kind of marshmallow magic, a charm to give you confidence.

What you sing doesn't matter – you could warble a lullaby or a rap song or the theme tune to a TV ad (last night my choice happened to be U2's "The Sweetest Thing" – it was on the VH1 music channel before I came upstairs). What's important when you're singing is that you concentrate on the vastness of the sky and the power of all those flickering, faraway planets.

What's *also* important is that unless you happen to be standing on the top of a mountain in the middle of nowhere, you can't sing *too* loud, or your neighbours will call the police and they'll come and charge you with Being Noisy and Demented.

"Your bag looks heavy," says Morven, as I sit down next to her and her pro-wrestling door angel in art class, placing my nearly-finished collage on the desk and my mini-rucksack on the floor (with a clunk).

"What've you got in it?" says Jade, eyeing it suspiciously.

"Nothing much," I lie. "Usual stuff."

Jade's dark, unfathomable eyes fix on me for what feels like for ever, but is probably more like a nanosecond. Then they flit down on to my bag, examining the strange bumps and bulges through the thin material of the bag. I have this funny feeling she has X-ray vision, like one of those machines at the airport.

I bet she already knows all my secrets. I bet she's reeling off all the contents of my bag in her detective-like mind:

- 1 pack of paper tissues (opened)
- 2 squashed paper tissues (used)
- 1 packet of Munchies (half-eaten)
- 1 Hello Kitty purse (not exactly bulging with money)
- 1 mobile phone (which Kyle Strachan *might* phone me on, one of these days, fingers and toes crossed)
- 1 blue velvet jewellery pouch (which the Luckenbooth originally came in) filled with rose petals from the bush in the back garden
- 1 bamboo box, bought from the Pound Shop in Aberdeen, hand-painted (yesterday) with fancy scrolls and the words "Rose" and "Rouge" on it, which contains: dice, a fossil, a piece of rose quartz, a tiny bell, an antique pot of blusher and the Loveheart sweet with "*YOU AND ME*" printed on it
- A snow dome (complete with a picture newly fitted in the empty slot).

Hey, I felt like I needed as much marshmallow magic as I could carry this morning. And so far it's worked – I haven't caught the slightest, toxic glimpse of Sian Ellis.

"Oh, yeah, I forgot!" I say, picking my bag up and rummaging inside it. "You always wanted to see a photo of Rose Rouge – well, here she is!"

"Oh, she's so pretty!" gasps Morven, as her and Jade lean over the desk and examine my sister's laughing face through a flurry of fake snow.

"She really looks like you!" says Jade. "And your mum a bit too!"

I might be a little hurt by Rose Rouge's unusual lack of contact right now, but I can't help feeling chuffed at being compared to the girl in the picture. Who wouldn't?

"I thought you said she had long dreadlocks? With bells and coloured threads wrapped around them and everything?"

Morven is holding the snow dome so close – examining the long, dark, shiny hair on show – that she's practically making herself go cross-eyed.

"It's an old photo. She's about sixteen there," I explain with a shrug. "She didn't have dreads then."

"Lemmie!"

I jump at the sound of that teacherly voice, thinking for a split-second that I'm back in Mrs O'Farrell's classroom and I'm about to get told off, *again*. But then if it had been Mrs O'Farrell, she'd have been calling me "Laurel", and that voice was too nice and friendly to be yelling at me to get to the head's office, *again*.

"Hope you don't mind, but I had a thought about your collage at the weekend," says Ms McIver, standing on the other side of the table wearing jeans and a stripy cap-sleeved T-shirt, accessorized with a wriggly puppy under her arm.

"Um . . . no! I don't mind – I think!"

As long as she's not going to tell me it sucks, of course, not when we're one day away from the exhibition for parents' night. . .

"Well, I was thinking about the circular window, and what you could use for it," Ms McIver continues, pointing a finger at the last white empty space on my cluttered collage. "And then I was cutting up a lemon and suddenly thought, *perfect*!"

As Harvey wriggles in one arm, Ms McIver uses her other hand to slip into her back pocket and bring out a slightly shrivelled but perfectly circular slice of lemon.

"I dried it out in the microwave. Didn't want to get your masterpiece all soggy!" she laughs.

I feel like laughing too, when I see how perfectly it fits the picture and how well it fits *me* (a lemon for Laurel Lemon). All I need is some glue, and my collage'll be –

Why is Morven nudging me under the table? And why is Harvey growling?

"Hey, hi, Laurel!"

It's like a dark thundercloud has slipped in front of the sun. A thundercloud dressed in a powder-pink T-shirt, matching pink flared jeans, a neat, perky ponytail and a warm, friendly smile.

"Oh!" gasps Ms McIver, turning and frowning at Sian Ellis, her heart probably pitter-pattering, thinking at first she'd been nabbed by someone important for harbouring an illegal (non) wild animal. "Er, can I help you?"

"Hi! I'm Sian – I started here yesterday."

Sian has been here at my school for just over a day now but already she's acting confident and relaxed, like she owns the place. *Wow*, I can't stand her.

"Ah, yes, you're the girl Mr Murray introduced in assembly," nods Ms McIver, visibly relaxing. "What can I do for you, Sian?"

Harvey is still growling. Everyone in class is enjoying a closer-up nosey at the new girl. Morven is pressing her knee hard against mine under the desk. I haven't said anything. I don't think I can *move*.

"I'm in the other art class just now, and Mr Roberts sent me through to ask if you've got any black poster paint he could borrow?" Sian asks brightly, her full-beam smile directed at Ms McIver.

"Harvey, *shush*! What's wrong with you? Anyway, yes – there should be a new bottle in the cupboard by the door. Help yourself on the way out. Oh, and can you knock next time you come to my classroom, Sian?"

At that minor telling off, just for the weeniest *flutter* of a second, I think I see Sian's smile slip. Or maybe I'm just imagining it. (Me, paranoid? What on *earth* could be making me feel paranoid?!)

"Yes, of course, miss. And bye, Laurel – we'll have to catch up later!" says Sian, as she spins around to leave.

Despite being shushed, Harvey keeps on growling. And despite been spoken to twice, I still can't say a thing to Sian.

"Have you two met already?" Ms McIver asks me, as soon as Sian has bounced out of our Portakabin and gone back to her own class.

"They were at the same primary school, back in Edinburgh," Jade jumps in and explains, maybe worrying that I've lost my voice in the last couple of minutes.

"Oh! An old friend? That must be nice for you, Lemmie!" says Ms McIver, a curious smile on her face, as she finally gives up on trying to hold on to Harvey and his wriggles and puts him down on the floor.

As soon as his four fat, short legs hit the lino, he's limping off towards the door, barking like crazy.

"Harvey! *What* have I told you about being quiet. . .?"

As Ms McIver hurries over to placate her puppy, Jade puts her hand on my shoulder and says, "You OK, Lem?"

"Absolutely!" I try to smile. "Ms McIver helped me finish my project early. Once I get this final bit glued down, I'll have the rest of the period free!"

Well, what's the point in trying to explain? Sian's here to stay, and the less I say about her and the less I have to do with her in person the better. All I can do is hope, hope, *hope* she doesn't start playing her mean games again, and hope, hope, *hope* no one falls for her whispers and lies this time around.

"Grrr. . ." growls Harvey, still clawing frantically at the Portakabin door, despite Ms McIver's stroking.

Hmm. They *say* animals have a sixth sense, don't they? In that case, maybe dopey little Harvey has sniffed out the snaggle-toothed, warty monster lurking under Sian's perfect skin. . . .

18

How to blow a second chance (big-time)

If I'd been a boy, my parents were going to call me "Orlando".

That's Latin for "bright sun", or American for "town right next to Disneyworld". Or Scottish for "ha, ha, ha – we're going to beat you up for having such a fancy-pants name!".

Hurrah, phew, thank goodness etc. that I was a girl, and my parents ended up calling me Laurel, which just means (boringly but safely) "a kind of tree". Even if I changed it to something altogether more fruity somewhere down the line.

But I've always been fascinated by names, which is why I thought hard about what to call my pet house-mouse. Last night – as it crept slowly, warily closer to the crumb I was holding out to it – I tried out some cute names (Titch, Midge, Peanut), and then a few joke names (Kylie, Jumbo, Elvis), before the right one finally dawned on me. . .

"'Craig'?! You're calling a mouse '*Craig*'?" says Jade, as we wander in a meandering crocodile with the rest of the class out of the Portakabin, across the sun-filled, tarmacked playground and towards the main school reception. We're all off to spend the next hour arranging our works of art on the walls, ready for the whole school's mums and dads to gasp at in wonder (or more likely *ignore*) when they shuffle in here for parents' night tonight.

"Awww, Craig the mouse . . . that's cute!" grins Morven (which means "child of the sea", by the way), while Jade ("semi-precious gemstone") just looks bewildered.

"Yeah, Craig. After the Craigandarroch Lodge," I explain, as I hold my collage out in front of me very, *very* carefully. (Morven, meanwhile, is dangling her pro-wrestling, non-delicate door angel by one chunky leg.)

I'd been thinking about the Craigandarroch Lodge just before the mouse had come scrabbling up beside me, lured out of hiding by the buttery piece of toast I'd been eating. The reason I'd been thinking about the Lodge was 'cause all this week there's been ominous booming and thunkings coming from that side of town, as the old solid building is thumped and bashed into rubble. The last couple of days after school I'd thought about going up to check out the damage, and both days, the very idea had just made me feel kind of blue. . .

"Hey, look, Lemmie!" says Jade, nudging me so hard that I nearly scrunch my collage. "There's *Kyle*!"

(Kyle: "handsome and lovely". How appropriate. . .)

It *is* Kyle, on the way – like the rest of his class – to his art lesson. Our class, laden down with our masterpieces, were all allowed out of our last period's French lesson a little bit early so we could sort out our mini-exhibition. (Don't know how Ms McIver wangled *that* with Mrs Fraser the French teacher – promised her a cuddle of Harvey, maybe?)

"He's waving at you! *Again!*" giggles Morven.

I can see that. I only hope Kyle can't quite see how pink my cheeks have gone (fat chance). It's hard to wave back when you're holding an easily crinkled collage, so instead I just nod and grin (and blush) at him.

"Hey, Lem," mutters Jade. "Kyle's not the *only* one waving at you . . . check it out!"

Trailing not far behind Kyle, but with no one in particular keeping her company, is Sian Ellis. She's smiling at me and wiggling her fingers in my direction. I nearly miss the first of the steps up to reception, and might've gone flying if Jade hadn't caught me by the elbow.

"That Sian girl, she looked a bit lonely, didn't she?" says Morven, glancing back as Sian and the rest of her class disappear from view.

Oh, please don't start feeling sorry for her! I whisper silently, leaving fingerprint indents on the edges of my collage, I'm suddenly gripping it so tightly.

"Mmm," mutters Jade, "I guess you've got to feel sorry for her in a way – it *is* tough when you first start at a new school. And maybe she's smiling, but I bet that's just 'cause she's trying to hide how nervous she feels."

Please, please don't let this be happening all over again. Carys said exactly the same thing when Sian started at Sunnybank. . .

"Hey, Lem – I know you said Sian was a pain at your old school – all snobby and up herself," says Morven, holding the glass door of the main entrance open for me. "But I was thinking maybe she'll be different now she's here in Balgownie. . .?"

I give a minuscule shrug in reply, too spaced out to speak.

"Maybe Morv's right. Maybe now Sian's away from her old crew, she'll be a bit less of a big-head, and be a lot nicer – you never know!"

I want to tell Jade that I suspect there's as much chance of Sian being nicer as there is of sharks turning vegetarian, or axe murderers in horror movies getting into basket-weaving instead of random slaughtering.

As far as my trusting mates are concerned, maybe it seems like a case of so far, so nice with Sian, but I wouldn't trust her as far as I could throw her. (And ideally that would be all the way back to Edinburgh. . .)

"I don't know . . . maybe Sian deserves a second chance?" says Jade, her dark eyes boring into mine. "But you know her better than we do, Lemmie. What do *you* think?"

I think that is as insane an idea as leaving a kitten in the same room as a crocodile and expecting them to play nicely. I think I might be so scared of history repeating itself that I can't quite think of an answer to Jade's question. I think—

"Everybody SHUT UP now, please!" yells Ms McIver now we're all inside the foyer.

Thank goodness I've got something else to concentrate on, before Detective Inspector Jade Song notices that I'm gently flipping out and starts interrogating me.

"Right!" Ms McIver grins at us. "Let's try and get all the artworks up nice and quickly, OK?"

"OK!" we all mumble back.

Ms McIver, I suddenly can't help noticing, looks strangely nude right now without a puppy tucked under her arm or scampering around her Birkenstocks. But while we're here, Harvey is guarding the Portakabin (or probably just having forty doggy winks since there's no one around to fuss over him).

"Right, let's get this done!" says our ever-enthusiastic teacher.

But as Ms McIver points us all off to spots around the various walls and fires off directions, I can't help thinking about something Jade just said.

"Maybe Sian deserves a second chance. . .?"

Absolutely no *way* does Sian "deserve" a second chance. But maybe . . . maybe the only way I can survive Sian Ellis being here for a whole year is if I *do* give her a second chance. I *don't* mean I'll suddenly invite her round for tea/to Jade's party on Saturday/to be my new best buddy; it's just that if I *try* and smile a little bit, and *try* to say the odd word to her, it might be safer.

'Cause if I'm nice to her when she's got nobody, then maybe there's less chance of her turning on me again. Or spilling any of the secrets she knows about me.

Right. OK. I'll give this second chance thing a go.

Even if the very thought of it is already bringing me out in a really bad rash. . .

"You know what Shonagh just said to me?" Jade fumes, steam practically coming out of her ears.

"What?"

I want to give Jade my full attention, but my lemon-slice window has just fallen off my collage.

"She said my painting was just an ad for my granny and grandad's restaurant!"

It's hard to know how to answer that, because Jade's very well painted picture really *does* look like an advert for The Jade Palace. She might as well have stuck a menu up beside it; maybe some of the parents coming tonight could browse through it if they fancy going for a chow mein after they've found out how their kids are doing. . .

"She's just jealous," I say reassuringly, trying to think quickly of something else I can say to make her feel better. Maybe I should tell her that Shonagh's drawing of a magnificent stag looks more like a chubby donkey with a couple of twigs stapled to its forehead, but that seems a bit mean (though true).

"Oops! Bits of your collage trying to make a getaway, Lemmie?" says Ms McIver, pointing to my lemon window, which just looks like a bit of litter on the floor right now. "Think you'd better nip back to the classroom and get more glue!"

At least that gets me out of thinking up something to say to Jade.

I'll treat her to a Magnum on the way home to cheer her up, I decide as I barge out of the glass doors, skip down the steps and run around the corner of the building . . . where I stop dead.

'Cause there – outside the Portakabin that happens to be my art class – are Sian Ellis and Mr Murray. Sian is pointing inside the Portakabin and Mr Murray is patting her on the shoulder, as if she's been very, very good indeed.

Omigod! Harvey's in there, dreaming dreams of running through the heather snapping at bees once his leg is properly better. What can I do? What's Sian done? I don't know – all I know is that I panic, running as fast as my flip-flops will let me towards the main entrance. . .

"Lemmie?! What's wrong?" asks Ms McIver, but I'm too breathless and panicky to say anything.

Behind Ms McIver, I can see Morven and Jade and just about everyone else in my class turning one by one to stare my way.

"I . . . I . . ."

I actually can't handle the fact that they're all

staring like that, kind of puzzled and weirded out by me. It's too much like it used to be, back at Sunnybank. It just makes me start breathing faster and shallower, and the words seem even *harder* to get out.

"Lemmie! Calm down!" says Ms McIver gently, reaching out and holding on to my arms.

I'm shaking, I know I am. Part of that is because I know that Ms McIver's dog-shaped secret has been blown and partly because I know that Sian has done this deliberately, in revenge for Ms McIver telling her off for not knocking yesterday, and for Harvey growling at her.

And if Sian is capable of doing that, then there's no point me giving her a second chance.

And no point thinking I've got a hope in hell of her keeping her trap shut about me.

Goodbye, my lovely, sparkly, shiny new life, and hello misery, all over a—

"Ms McIver! Can I have a word, please?" Mr Murray's voice booms in the doorway behind me.

From the shocked look on my teacher's face – as well as everyone's in my class – I can tell that Mr Murray is holding Harvey. (The soft whining is a bit of a giveaway too.)

"Yes. Yes, of course, Mr Murray," Ms McIver mumbles sheepishly, letting go of my arms and walking towards her doom.

"I think we need to discuss why this dog has been in your classroom, and why this matter had to be brought to my attention by a pupil just now. . ."

As Mr Murray leads Ms McIver outside for a showdown, I can't stop shivering. That's 'cause all eyes are on me, shocked and accusing. Even Jade and Morven have stunned, quizzical expressions aimed my way.

Omigod. . .!

They all think *I'm* the pupil Mr Murray is talking about. . .!

19

Love and leis. . .

I can't breathe.

"What's the matter with Lemmie?" I hear Ms McIver demand worriedly.

"It's like she's having an asthma attack or something!" I hear Morven's anxious voice tell her.

"I think she's maybe hyperventilating," Jade says more precisely, her hand rubbing comforting but useless circles on my back.

Jade and Morven, they dragged me out of the foyer when they saw that I was having a panic-attack and got me to sit down here on the steps. I guess they thought the fresh air would help, but it hasn't. I'm still gasping and stressing and staring down between my knees without even seeing the grey asphalt my flip-flops are planted on.

"Jade, do me a favour – go inside and get everyone back to fixing up their artworks," Ms McIver orders gently. "And Morven, here are my car keys – can you put Harvey in my Mini for me? I'll look after Lemmie. Don't worry, she'll be all right."

All right?! The only way I'll be all right is if I manage to go home and persuade my parents to move immediately to Aberdeen or Aberystwyth or Argentina or somewhere.

"Take a slow, deep breath, Lemmie!"

I do as I'm told – even though fainting through lack of oxygen seems like an easy way out at the minute. At least I wouldn't have to look at all those accusing, disappointed faces again. . .

"Good! And another one!"

Ms McIver's hand on my back is doing a better job than Jade's; she's moving it slower, which seems to help calm down my breathing.

"That's more like it – and again, nice and slow. . ."

In the space of six breaths, my heart has stopped thundering and my lungs don't feel so much like they're wrapped tight in cling-film any more. It's just been Rainbow Breathing, I realize, without the rainbows. . .

"So, what's all this about, Lemmie?"

I bite my lip. Telling never does any good. Telling can get you into more trouble instead of *out* of it.

"Please, Lemmie – something got you upset. Was it because Mr Murray found Harvey?"

I shake my head.

"They all thought it was *me*. . ." I mumble.

"What – you mean the rest of the class thought *you* were to blame for Mr Murray finding out about Harvey?"

Nod, nod.

"But that's crazy – the head told me it was that new girl! She was returning the paint she borrowed yesterday, apparently, and that's how it happened," says Ms McIver. "Why she felt she had to report Harvey to Mr Murray I've *no* idea. . ."

My teacher's voice has an edge to it as she fades out.

"But Lemmie, why didn't you just tell them all, instead of getting yourself wound up? They're all your friends – they *know* you wouldn't have done something like that!"

Huh – I had friends in the past that I thought would believe me, and look what happened *then*. . .

"Listen," says Ms McIver, after giving me a few seconds to reply (I don't). "Here's what's going to happen. You're going to go to the loos and splash water on your face and sort yourself out – I'll get Jade to go with you. Then I'm going to go in there and say that a pupil from another class accidentally came across Harvey and blew the whistle. OK?"

"OK," I whisper.

At least Ms McIver hasn't backed Sian Ellis, like Mrs O'Farrell used to.

At least not *yet* . . . and for that small mercy all I can do is say "phew".

I can't breathe.

This time it's because Craig is sitting on my hand – *on my hand!* – nibbling a walnut.

And if you don't believe me, then ask Morven. Not that she can believe it either.

"Oooh!" she coos, watching Craig nervously nibbling on the all-too-tempting nut. "He's adorable! Or is he a she?"

"I don't know," I whisper, hardly daring to move. "I think I might need a very big magnifying glass to know that for sure!"

Craig might be here for the walnut, but Morven is here to have a last-minute party discussion. Which we should actually talk about some more, before my parents come home from parents' night and give Morven her promised lift back home. But so far we've had tea, watched some TV and talked about what happened this afternoon. (Ms McIver seemed to have explained stuff away to the class OK, which I was pleased about, though it would take me *ages* to shake the memory of those condemning stares out of my head.)

"So you really do like the decorations?" I ask her softly, as I try not to alarm Craig.

"Like 'em?! They're *brilliant*, Lemmie!"

Morven's enthusiasm is great, if you're me, but a bit too frightening, if you happen to be about the size of the walnut you're trying to eat.

"Oops. . ." says Morven, as Craig vanishes and I'm left with a large knobbly, nibbled nut in my hand.

"Doesn't matter," I reassure her. "Craig'll be back. Let's talk about the party!"

"OK!" nods Morven, who does look kind of cute with the five leis she has draped around her neck. "Well, everything's cool, isn't it?"

"Everyone's been invited?"

"Yep," nods Morven, picking up another lei from the pile and looping it around her wrist as a bracelet.

"And everyone knows what to wear?"

I'd already suggested the dress code – anything that looks like a naff tourist outfit, with no entry unless you a) look naff enough and b) are wearing sunglasses.

"Yep – I told everyone."

"Cool. And Jade's mum and dad are still all right about pretending they're taking her to Aberdeen for the day?"

Morven got her mum to sort this out with Jade's parents. They were going to get Jade in the car at five-to-four on Saturday afternoon (pretending they were on their way to some fancy pizza restaurant in Aberdeen as a birthday treat) then they'd drive five minutes along the road to Morven's place and – surprise! – drop her off at her party.

"Absolutely," Morven nods again. "There's just one tiny, wee, *minuscule* hiccup. . ."

Uh-oh. I've had enough horrible surprises today.

"What sort of hiccup?" I ask, worriedly, feeling the flickerings of my worry-rash prickling on my skin again.

"Well, I haven't been *totally* able to sort out the food. . ."

OK, so Morven had taken on more than me: I'd been in charge of coming up with a theme and making the decorations. But Morven had seemed fine about doing her share: inviting everyone and doing the catering.

"*What*? But I thought you said you and your mum were on to it! I thought you were going to look on the net for Hawaiian recipes!" I say in a panic.

"Well, *yeah* . . . but Mum just sort of freaked out when she saw the recipes – it was all stuff like 'cook the fish with the coconut and banana'. You know Mum; her sort of thing is more chocolate cake and sticky-toffee pudding."

Fair enough – I had only eaten brilliant but not-exactly-exotic food round at Morven's. But how was I to know that Morven's mum would come over all dyslexic when she was looking at menus that weren't particularly Scottish, or British?

"So what are we going to do *now*?" I ask, feeling as panicked as Craig did when he heard Morven bellow "*brilliant!*". "The party's on Saturday – are we going to have to ask all the guests to bring their own packets of crisps?"

"Don't worry!" Morven tries to reassure me, though it's hard to take her seriously when she's swamped in paper flowers. "Mum's still making lots of cakes and stuff, but she spoke to Jade's parents, and Jade's grandparents have offered to do all the Hawaiian themed food. Only in a Chinese sort of style. . ."

I can't help getting the giggles (in a nervous, ever-so-slightly hysterical way). Jade's surprise party is looking like it might be a surprise for Jade in *lots* of ways. Like:

1) She isn't expecting a party.

2) Especially a Hawaiian luau of a party.

3) Where everyone has been asked to come dressed like a corny tourist (shades compulsory).

4) And all the food is, er, Chinese (apart from mountains of cake and shortbread Morven's mum will serve up).

"Well, fine!" I laugh.

The sillier the party the better. In fact, I think I like the idea of a Hawaiian/Chinese/Scottish themed party better than anything I could've come up with. And more than anything right now, I need a party to cheer me up. (Actually, more than anything, I need to speak to Rose Rouge, but she's still being ominously quiet. . .)

"Yeah!" Morven laughs too, taking a lei off the pile and aiming it at my head. "It'll be fun!"

We're both cracking up at the fact that the lei has flown past my head and landed in the bin when the door of my bedroom bursts open.

Er . . . what happened to knock-knock? And why didn't Isla do her bouncer act and keep trouble away from my door?

"Oh . . . Morven," says Dad, with Mum hovering behind him on the stairs. They're both looking a bit confused, as if they'd totally forgotten Morven would be here, even though they already knew she was staying for tea and had said earlier that they'd run her home after they got back from school.

"Um, hi, Mr Ferguson! Mrs Ferguson!" Morven mutters, looking from both of them to me with a puzzled frown.

(Hey, don't look at *me*, I feel like saying. *I* don't know what's going on.)

"Um . . . ready for your lift home, Morven?" says Dad, giving Mum a funny look.

"Sure!"

Morven unravels the flowery twists of lei from round her neck and wrists quicker than you can say "weird atmosphere" and is waving me bye as she leaves.

And speaking of leaving, I'm left with Mum, who's glancing around my room for somewhere to sit down, as if the place is as comfy as a hotbed of molten lava.

"So. . ." she says finally, as she settles herself down in the middle of the carpet, with the mounds of decorations for Jade's party stacked up all around her.

"So?" I repeat.

I don't know what I expected after the parents' night, but it certainly isn't this. I'm pretty sure that all my teachers quite like me – even Mr Guthrie, who makes me do all those science experiments – so I can't see any of them giving me a bad report. And I even sort of hoped Mum and Dad would have something nice to say about my (superglued) bit of artwork in the foyer.

The way the corner of Mum's mouth is twitching and the way she's repeatedly tucking her hair behind her ears, I don't think there's good news or a compliment coming. . .

"Ms McIver –"

Ms McIver?! What did Ms McIver have to say that would make Mum and Dad this weird? Isn't art my best, most *favourite* subject? Hadn't Jade pointed out that Ms McIver had placed my collage in the most prominent, prized position, right by the doors into the hall?

I don't feel like making it easy for Mum, so instead of saying anything, I stare at her, while sticking my hand into my jeans pocket and letting my fingers slip around the silky smoothness of today's feather (a pheasant's).

"Ms McIver said you were very jumpy and agitated today, Laurel. She said you're a wonderful pupil, and a pleasure to teach normally. But a couple of times this week you've acted a little . . . odd?" Mum gazes at me with eyes that say "tell me".

But how can I tell her? How can I tell her that the only time I've ever acted odd during this whole nearly-year at Balgownie Academy was when Sian Ellis reared her ponytailed head?

Why would she believe me *this* time round, since she certainly didn't seem to *last* ti—

"*EEEEEEEEEEEEEEEEEEEEEEEEEEEEEEEEEEE. . .!*"

Uh-oh.

Mum and Craig have just made eye-contact.

Something tells me it's *not* love at first sight.

". . .*EEEEEEEEEEEEEEEEEEEEEEEEEEK!!*"

"Mum! It's OK!" I try and tell her while she jumps to her feet, skidding over paper and backing her way a couple of steps to the door.

Craig – beating his own retreat – is nowhere to be seen.

"How can you say it's OK, Lemmie?" she pants. "We've spent a fortune on this house – we can't have it overrun by rodents!"

Sometimes Mum is so cool, and sometimes she disappoints me so much. Why can't she just love this house for what it is, and not what it looks like and what it's worth?

"Mum, it's only one tiny mouse! You can't exactly say we're being 'overrun'!"

"Lemmie – don't be cheeky. It doesn't suit you!"

I feel like I've been slapped across the face by that comment. *She's* the one who's acting hysterical – I was only trying to point out how dumb it was to overreact.

"I was *not* being cheeky!" I tell her, blinking back hot, hurt tears.

"Oh, I'm sorry, Lemmie, I didn't mean it like that," says Mum, coming towards me with her arms outstretched. "I'm just a bit . . . well, it was just when your teacher said that your behav—"

I push myself back on the bed and as far away from her as possible.

"Don't . . . just *don't* start accusing me of having 'behavioural problems' – *again!*"

Now it's Mum's turn to look a bit tearful. She's opening her mouth to say something, then seems to change her mind.

In a second, she's gone, pulling the door shut behind her.

I give it a second to make sure she's safely downstairs, then I get down on my hands and knees, frantically checking the skirting boards in the direction Craig scuttled off in.

There it is – a tiny hole . . . an old knot in the wood that's come loose. It's just the right size to fit a finger (or a small mouse) through.

And now I'm about to shove something else through – supplies.

"Look, I don't want to block you behind here," I say to Craig, hoping he's somewhere just behind the boards, and can miraculously understand human-babble. "But if Mum sees you running about in my room again, she'll probably put mousetraps down."

As I talk, I break the walnut I just found on the floor into bits and stuff them through to the far side of the wall with the end of my pencil.

"And hey – I've got something else!" I mutter, rummaging in my school bag and finding the fluff-covered Munchies that have been mouldering in there underneath all my marshmallow magic paraphernalia.

It's messier and harder to break up a couple of munchies but getting my fingers covered in toffee and chocolate is a small price to pay for Craig's safety.

"Check it out – we can still see each other!" I whisper, as I take the rose quartz out of the box in my bag and get ready to put the pointier end of it in the knothole. "It'll be like a stained-glass window!"

As I stick it in place, I get down on my elbows and imagine the view from Craig's side. I hope it doesn't make him too sad to stare through and see a rose-tinted version of my room, with a rose-tinted me mooching about in it. It makes me feel pretty sad – I hardly knew him but he was my first, almost pet ever. If you didn't count the dog that –

Uh-oh. . . I didn't hear Dad come in downstairs. But I can make out some whispered shouting going on. I don't want to hear what they're saying. I want to get into bed and curl myself small.

The smaller I am,
the less easy it'll be for problems
to find me.

"Lemmie? Can I come in?"

It's Dad, peering warily around the door.

"No."

"But Lemmie, maybe we should talk. . ."

"No. Please leave me alone."

I'm not looking directly at him, but I can see from the corner of my eye that Dad – like Mum – is about to say something and then stops himself.

"Please – I just want to be on my own," I tell him again.

"OK. Maybe we can talk tomorrow?"

I don't say anything and can just make out Dad leaving, pulling the door closed till the catch clicks softly.

And so it's just me and the butterflies on my walls.

I don't have the energy to get up and grab my mobile to call Rose Rouge. I don't have the energy to listen to her jokey answering message, or wait for her to call me back, which will probably be sometime next *year*, the way things are going.

I wish I had the energy to call out to Dad and tell him I was a big, fat liar.

Of *course* I didn't want to be left on my own. . .

20

Long-lashed shark eyes

At some point last night, with the lights and my clothes still on – and paper butterflies dancing behind my closing eyelids – I fell asleep.

And wake up this morning feeling . . . OK.

Well, just about.

The sun blazing in through the skylight helps me feel a glimmer of shininess; it makes my room light up like I have a real live rainbow living in it.

And so I get up and put on my current favourite clothes: the cherry tie-dyed T-shirt, my green baggy trousers with sequinned pink flowers twisting up one leg, and my red velvet Chinese pumps. Then I dig out a handful of butterfly-shaped diamanté hair-clips, and pin my hair up on just one side with all five of them.

My marshmallow magic stuff; it's still packed in my bag from yesterday, but for a bit of extra protection, I stop as I go to leave my room and decide to give Isla an outing just this once, for old times' sake. As I stuff her in my trouser pocket, I hitch my (heavy) bag on to my shoulder and blow a kiss towards the rose quartz window in the skirting board, half-imagining Craig sitting behind it, munching on a Munchie and waving a toffee-covered paw back at me.

Luck seems to be with me when I pad downstairs – looks like Dad has already left to go to a job and Mum is on the phone, talking loudly to someone about Swedish kitchen units or something just as dull. So I manage to sneak out the door without any awkward discussions or just-as-awkward silences.

Because I've left so early for school, I take the long way round, past Craigandarroch – I've been putting off peeking at the damage for too long. But now I'm here there's nothing to see . . . unless you count dust-covered lorries rumbling in and out of towering mesh gates. Behind the metal fencing that'd first ringed the Lodge and the woods, there's now blank, bland wooden hoardings, roughly painted white.

"So much for the wish me and Jade made in the fairy circle," I mumble, above the sounds of drills and hammering.

There are still trees towering above the cheap and tacky hoardings, but for how long? For all I know, half the woods behind there have been flattened already, along with the Lodge and the fairy circle, of course. To check on that, I'll have to climb up to the top of Craigandarroch hill and look down but even that's going to be tricky, since the main path to the hill is blocked off by the fencing now. I'll have to take the long way around, via the windier, more overgrown path that you can get to from the playing fields. . .

But that'll have to wait till another day.

For now, I turn away, and start walking towards school, kind of wishing I hadn't bothered coming, since it's sort of rubbed some of the shininess off my morning. . .

Uh-oh – I've just noticed I've got a little memento of Craigandarroch: powdery white building dust all over my velvet pumps.

I lean on a Mini in the staff section of the school car park, while I lift one foot up and brush the worst of the dust away.

The owner of the Mini won't mind – it belongs to Ms McIver. (I'd never *dream* of leaning on Mr Murray's car – that would feel like crossing some invisible, no-go line. It would be like asking him if he wants to play Pooh sticks on the bridge after school one day, or if he fancies going halfers on an extra-long ice-pole with you.)

"*HmmmMMMmmmm-mmmmmMMMmmm!*"

How weird.

"*HmmmMMMmmmm-mmmMMMmmm!*"

Where's that strange, tuneless whiny whine coming from?

"*HmmmmmMMMMmm!*"

Scrabble, scrabble, scrabble.

"*Hmmmmmm-MMmmmmmm!*"

And then I see him – a bundle of big-eyed puppy, his paws scrambling at the window of the car to get my attention.

"Hello, Harvey!" I say, wriggling my fingers through the few centimetres' gap at the top of the car window.

Ms McIver must have left that open so Harvey has plenty of air. And I guess she's chosen to have him in the car 'cause at least then she can keep darting out between classes to keep an eye on the bandages he still needs to wear, and not chew off. . .

Harvey's scratchy wet tongue licks frantically at my hand, his injured tail flapping in high speed circles, as he gazes up hopefully at me.

"Oh, I'm sorry . . . but I can't let you out! You're not allowed to play with us any more!"

Glancing into the car, I see that Ms McIver has tried to make Harvey as comfortable as possible. Apart from parking in the shade and leaving the window a little bit open, she's put a big bowl of water and another of crunchies in the footwell, and there's a fluffy blankie on the back seat with a ton of squeaky toys to play with.

But Harvey doesn't want that – he wants human company. He wants to be back in the Portakabin, getting his head patted and his tummy tickled by all Ms McIver's more-than-willing students. And he'd *still* be doing that, if a certain Sian Ellis hadn't spoiled it for everyone (human and canine).

"Poor puppy. . ." I mumble, as Harvey leaps up and tries to nuzzle my fingers with his wet nose.

"*Grrrrrr. . .*"

Um, I wasn't expecting that. What's got into Harvey all of a sudd –

And then I see her reflection in the car window. She's standing right behind me, smirking.

I give myself half a second before I turn round – which is long enough to do a quick bit of marsh-mallow magic. ("Just imagine you're in *Star Trek* or something," Rose Rouge once told me, "and you're wearing this protective spacesuit that nothing can get through. Not radiation, not bullets, *nothing*.")

Slowly, I swivel to face Sian, staring at her still-smirking face through the pretend visor of my pretend helmet.

"Hey . . . who'd have guessed we'd end up at the same school again?" she says brightly. "When Dad told me we'd be moving to Balgownie for a year, I said, yay!, that's where Sammi said her mum had heard you'd moved to!"

Something's not right here, I think, within my safety bubble. *She's acting too nice.*

But then I spot that it's for Jenna Harris and Shonagh Robertson's benefit: the two of them are strolling very close to us, checking us both out inquisitively.

"Hi, Lemmie! Hi, er, Sian!" says Shonagh, as they pass by.

"Hi. . ." I smile and wave back, wishing I had the guts to push by Sian and go and join Shonagh and Jenna. Either that, or just shout "Help!".

"Hi!" Sian calls out, flashing her brightest, whitest smile at the girls before turning back to me. She's still smiling, as her long-lashed shark eyes scan me and what I'm wearing from feet to head and back again, ready to pronounce her judgement.

"So, freak-girl – you're looking . . . ridiculous!" she laughs.

Ah, now, *this* is more what I'm used to from her.

Snidey, nasty, pointed little digs out of listening range of any witnesses.

"Actually, *I* think you've got worse, haven't you? It was bad enough that time when you came to school and tried to customize the uniform. D'you remember?"

Of course I remember. And even if I'd tried to forget it, it sounded like Sian was about to remind me. How very helpful of her. . .

"Instead of black tights, you wore those horrible black and yellow stripy ones. And you came carrying a bunch of daffodils. You had a daffodil in the lapel of your blazer too, *and* one stuck in your hair. You looked terrible; like a cross between a bee and a *prat*."

If I'm in a pretend space-age suit, maybe I could have a pretend laser gun too. I point the index finger of the hand that's resting on my bag and blast a pretend beam at Sian. Nothing happens. She doesn't even stammer over her next mean words.

"And what's with everyone calling you 'Lemmie'? What kind of stupid nickname is that?" she asks, keeping a pleasant, half-smiling expression on her face so that anyone watching would just assume she was asking where the loos were, or what was safe to eat at school dinners.

I say nothing. What is there to say? ("Hey, Sian, I

was *so* bored with everything being brilliant here – I'm *so* glad you've come to Balgownie to shake things up a bit for me. . .!")

"My God!" she suddenly gasps.

Yes! Did my pretend laser gun just have a delayed action?

Er, no. . .

"I can't believe you're *still* carrying that ratty doll around with you!" Sian says this in the prettiest of girlie voices, that would sound sort of delighted to anyone not listening too closely to the actual words. "How old do you think you are, Laurel – *five*? And I thought I got rid of that for you *long* ago!"

I quickly shove Isla deeper into my trouser pocket out of sight, in case she's traumatized (like me) by the memory of the flushing incident.

"Oh, and I've been *dying* to ask, Laurel – what does everyone think of having a real, live loony like you at their school?"

I make a mistake and look shocked, like she's been able to penetrate the impenetrable spacesuit. Sian sees the flicker of hurt on my face and hers lights up.

"Oh, *I* get it! They don't know, do they? *How* funny! I mean, I can hardly believe they think you're normal, the way you're dressed and everything. Same goes for those stupid marks you're still drawing on your arm."

Argghhh. I hadn't stopped for a shower this morning – I hadn't wanted to get caught by Mum and Dad. And I didn't realize I'd been sleep-doodling again.

"Tell you what, Laurel!" says Sian, clapping her hands together as if she's about to suggest we do something cutesy-nice like go on a teddy bears' picnic together. "I promise not to tell everyone at school how insane you really are, if you do me a favour. Do you want to hear what that favour is?"

I can't speak, I can't move, I can't run – I'm weighed down by that heavy hunk of stone that seems to have appeared in my stomach again.

"I'll take that as a yes," Sian says brightly. "So the deal is, I need new friends, and it's going to be a *lot* easier and quicker for me to get new friends if you go around telling everyone how nice or cool I am or whatever. Get it?"

Briiiinnnngggggg!!!!

The shrill of the bell has never sounded so good.

"Lemmie?"

It's Jade's voice – she's veering through the staff cars towards us.

"Think about it, Laurel, yeah?" Sian calls out over her shoulder as she walks away. "We can talk more about you helping me with my project . . . yeah?"

And with that she gives me a warm – fake – grin, and a friendly – phoney – wave bye.

"What was she on about?" Jade asks, frowning up at me now she's by my side.

For some reason, Jade suddenly reminds me of Lucy Liu out of *Charlie's Angels*; she looks stern enough to deliver a killer karate chop to anyone who crosses her path. I wish I dared to tell Jade the truth, and then she'd maybe turn those lethal weapon hands of hers on Sian. . .

"Um . . . she was saying she might need some help with some geography project she's doing," I shrug, ducking out of telling all again.

Jade doesn't believe me. I can tell because she won't stop staring at me. But then I guess I should have picked a subject I was actually good at, and I might have had a better chance of fooling her. . .

"But why would you want to help her, Lemmie? You said you didn't like her much, and after all, she snitched on Ms McIver yesterday, didn't she?"

Uh-oh. Jade has that same confused expression on her face, like she's finding it hard to figure me out. Which is only a couple of stages away from deciding I'm a weirdo. . .

"No . . . course I'm not going to help her. That's . . . that's what I was going to tell her, when the bell rang just now."

Relieved at getting out of that touchy conversation, I turn to wave bye-bye to Harvey, who's now hunkered in the driver's seat, all squidgy, adorable and forlorn.

As me and Jade turn and hurry towards the school entrance, I glance above the building at the towering mound of Craigandarroch hill.

Up at the top there, the green of the trees and the ferns are muddled together with splodges of purple heather and bright yellow broom. The sky is such a bright Mediterranean blue and so cloudless it makes me wonder if you could almost smell the sea from up there, brought over in the breeze from the faraway coast.

I wish, I wish, I *wish* I could grab Harvey and run up to the top of the hill with him, away from Balgownie, where everything's starting to be tinged with grey, thanks to Sian Ellis's gentle poisoning. . .

21

How to (pretend to) be brave

I got a lucky break last night (hey, I think someone, somewhere owed me one).

There was a panicked message from Mum, saying she and Dad were still at some new housing development in Banchory. They had a show flat to finish decorating before the place opened to the public at the weekend, and they were way, *way* behind, thanks to blah, blah, blah.

I tuned out of the rant about electricians and tuned back in when I heard her say they'd be stuck there till at least eleven tonight, maybe twelve. Would I be able to fix myself something to eat? (Yes, I wasn't four years old.) Would I be OK? (Yes, I'd be great – 'cause we wouldn't be able to have our dreaded "little chat" about my "behaviour" and our current "vermin" infestation after all.)

And so I spent the evening in front of the telly, watching rubbish, finishing the decorations for Jade's party, and trying to switch my brain to "off". I kind of managed to make it happen, except when my mobile rang and I thought it was Rose Rouge, but it was only Jade, saying hi, how was I, I'd been quiet all day. ("Felt like my funny bug might be back, that's all," I'd lied to her.)

I'd been well asleep by the time Mum and Dad finally arrived home. Well, not totally asleep, but I pretended to be when one of them – didn't open my eyes to see which one – squeaked my door open and peeked in on me.

There was no whispered shouting after that. My parents were probably just relieved that their mad daughter hadn't set the house on fire with sparklers or whatever while they were out. . .

"No! Absolutely not! I need that delivery *today*!" I hear Mum's voice drift out of the office as I attempt to sneak out of the house for the second morning running. "No: it *has* to be today. Tomorrow's Saturday, and that'll be too late! Look, I don't need excuses; I need delivery of— Oh, can you hold on a sec?"

Just as I'm about to get to the front door and make a bolt for freedom, Mum comes rushing out of the office with her hand held over the phone.

"Laurel! *Please* don't go! Let me finish this call, and then we can talk before you go to school!"

"I've got to go, Mum."

I can't look at her, I've got my hand on the latch.

"Laurel – please, what's going on with you? You look so unhappy! Can't you tell me what's going on?"

"I'm OK," I lie. Or maybe I'm not so much lying as keeping secrets. Lying; keeping secrets . . . it's hard to tell them apart sometimes, isn't it?

"But you're not OK, are you, darling! Your art teacher said –"

"Look, I just haven't been feeling well! I had a bug this week, remember?!"

"It's not just this week though. Things were starting to get sort of . . . a bit odd *last* week. I mean, you've started sleepwalking again, haven't you? Your dad found you sitting on the stairs one night, making marks on your arms with a felt-tip pen, just like you used to do back in Edinburgh. He had to lead you back to bed."

He did? I don't even remember, but I'm keeping my face so blank that Mum doesn't spot that.

"And then there was the business with the sparkler. What was all that about?"

"I was just fooling around, that's all!" I try to insist.

Mum's not convinced.

"Is it . . . is it something to do with Rory Ellis and his family moving here?"

My cheeks turn traitorously pink on me, giving a sliver of my secret away.

"His daughter being here in Balgownie; is it bringing back bad memories for you, Laurel? About all your problems, I mean?"

Mum – as ever – gets it *nearly* right, and then veers off to completely wrong.

Doesn't she *get* it, won't she *ever* get that *Sian* is the bad memory, that *Sian* is the problem?

I want to change the subject. I just want to get away and go to school – even though I don't really, since today's the day Sian is going to come looking for me to talk over the emotional blackmail she's got planned for me. And how can I say no to her? Even when I know that telling everyone how gorgeous and lovely and fluffy Sian is is going to make me *choke*. . .

"I've got to go," I mumble, not meeting Mum's gaze.

"Hello, Mrs Ferguson – are you still there? Hello?" a voice says fuzzily down the phone in Mum's hand.

She glances worriedly at it, and then back to me.

"Laurel – me, you and your dad have to sit down and talk about this. But we can't do it tonight, or tomorrow morning, because if we don't meet this deadline on the show flats, we don't get paid. So how about tomorrow afternoon, hmm? Just the three of us. Maybe we could go for a drive if it's nice, take a picnic and just spend some ti—"

"Mrs Ferguson! Can you hear me? Are we still connected?"

"Can't tomorrow afternoon – it's Jade's surprise party." I shrug and go to turn the latch.

"Hello? Hello?"

"OK – well, Sunday, then?"

Sunday's a couple of days away; I'll worry about that later. I've got more important things to worry about today. . .

"Mrs Ferguson! MRS FERGUSON!"

"Uh . . . Laurel, I've got to take this work call. . ."

Fine by me, I think. It means I can leave. . .

"But listen, till we get a chance to talk properly, if something *is* bothering you," says Mum, anxiously, holding on to my arm gently as I start to step outside the front door into the morning sunshine. "If it helps . . . maybe you should think what Rose Rouge would do in the same situation?"

I think that might just be the best advice my mum's ever given me. . .

So what would Rose Rouge do?

I know *exactly* what Rose Rouge would do. . .

"OK, so while she's inside," says Morven, nodding at Jade, who's in the café getting us some Friday afternoon, end-of-the-week, celebration Soleros, "I just wanted to ask, d'you fancy coming round to mine about ten-ish tomorrow morning?"

Morven is talking about getting the barn decorated in time for the official party kick-off at four. I'm listening, but over her shoulder I can see Sian Ellis strolling towards us, clutching her cute pink Ellesse bag in front of her, a sickly smile on her face. She's looking straight at me – while she talks to Jack McLennan, Iain Whyte and (gulp) Kyle Strachan.

"I've got a bit of a hassle," I tell Morven. "Mum and Dad are working tomorrow morning and I've got *loads* of stuff to take around to yours."

I'm trying to act normal. I can't let it show on my face that I *hate* it that Sian is anywhere *near* Kyle.

"Not a problem!" says Morven, unaware of what I'm looking at. "I'll ask Mum or Dad to come round and pick you up if you like. Oh, hold on – Jade's waving me to come in. They haven't run out of Soleros *again*, have they? Back in a sec. . ."

It's like it's meant to be. As Morven disappears inside the café to make a snap-decision second-choice, Kyle and his friends peel away from Sian, giving her a wave bye – and me a wave hi. . .

"That Kyle's pretty cute, isn't he?" smiles Sian, stopping right beside me.

I can sense that her evil alien antennae is up, registering the fact that Kyle's broad grin is aimed at me. So she can't have told him anything too bad about me *yet*, I guess. . .

"Kyle? Yeah, I s'pose he's all right," I say half-heartedly, playing down the fact that I think Kyle's pretty much wonderful.

It suddenly occurs to me that it's the first time I've actually been able to say anything directly to Sian in the whole of the week that she's been at our school.

But now it's time to play "pretend" again. Not pretend, protective *Star Trek* spacesuits, but pretend-I'm-Rose-Rouge. Pretend I'm this smart, confident, funny person who's never, *ever* going to let a slimy, pathetic bully like Sian Ellis think she's got the better of me. . .

"So what do you think, then?" Sian smirks prettily at me, just in case all the older kids currently sitting in booths in the café happen to be checking out her "loveliness". "About what I was saying yesterday? We should get together properly, figure out how it'll work and what you should tell people about me."

Red. . .

[breathe]

and yellow. . .

[breathe]
and pink...
[breathe]
and green....
[breathe]
orange...
[breathe]
and purple...
[breathe]
and blue...

I stare steadily at Sian, as I settle my nerves with a bit of Rainbow Breathing and tune into Rose Rouge. ("Bullies are cowards, Lemmie – sometimes you've just got to stand up to them. Mainly because they don't expect you to!")

"Laurel? Did you hear what I just said?" Sian says impatiently, even though you wouldn't guess it from the serene expression on her face.

"Yeah ... I'm just ignoring you, that's all," I say, flatly. "Thing is, I don't want to help you, and so I'm not going to help you. You want me to lie to everyone and pretend you're OK? I don't *think* so!"

Sian's face turns from butter-wouldn't-melt to I-want-to-kill-you-*now*.

But because Jade and Morven come back out of the café that very second, she has to back off, tail between her legs.

"See you later, Laurel!" Sian trills at me, probably to keep her cover in front of Morven and Jade. "Have a nice weekend!"

"What did *she* want?" asks Jade, handing me my Solero-substitute.

"Nothing," I say confidently, still feeling the courage of Rose Rouge flooding my veins.

Hey, I'll probably feel like nervy Lemmie Ferguson again by Monday morning. But for this weekend at least, I can enjoy acting like someone (someone like Rose Rouge) who's a thousand times more chilled out and confident than little old me.

I can't *wait* to tell Rose Rouge all about it. . .

22

To tell or not to tell

"It looks . . . mental!"

I know Morven means that in a good way, but considering the threats Sian was making a couple of days ago about spilling my past history, it's kind of sickly funny.

Only Morven doesn't know that – it's just one of my (many) secrets.

The "mental" Morven mentioned refers to the decorations dangling from the beams in the barn. From up here on the stepladder, as I pin the last end of the last paper flower garland in place, I have to admit they are pretty "mental", or great or whatever, even if I say it myself.

"It's like . . . it's like being in Kew Gardens!" Morven sighs, though she's never been to the world-famous Kew Gardens in London, or even London for that matter.

Not that I can speak. I've never been to London or Kew Gardens either, but I have been to the Winter Gardens in Aberdeen's Duthie Park, where tropical flowers trail and twist above you as you walk through the endless, giant, baking-hot Victorian greenhouses. If I've managed to do the faintest hint of a paper copy of that, I'll be pretty pleased. . .

"It's going to be a brilliant party, isn't it, Lemmie?" Morven beams up at me.

"Definitely," I tell her.

How could it not be? Morv's dad has borrowed a couple of long, folding function tables from the Balgownie golf club, and they're parked down one side of the barn, with the sound system Morven's dad also borrowed from the golf club's function suite placed on one of them. Then there's my pile of hand-made leis to welcome everyone when they arrive (in four hours' time), and tons of room for all the cakes Morv's mum is still frantically baking as we speak *and* the food that Jade's grandparents will be bringing over later, just before the birthday girl herself is deposited here by her mum and dad.

"Hey, you don't think Jade's guessed, do you?"

"Nah!" I shake my head at Morven's question, as I start stepping down from the ladder.

Actually, I wouldn't have been surprised if Jade had sussed something out – since she's so razor sharp – but when she called me last night for a chat, she didn't let anything slip. And she'd been happy enough to talk about seeing me and Morven on Sunday for a delayed birthday celebration (the line we'd spun her), since she'd be hanging out with her family all day Saturday (or so she thought).

"Y'know, Lemmie, you are so amazing at anything artistic!" says Morven now, grabbing a couple of leis off the pile and spinning them around her wrists.

"Um, thanks!" I blush Morven's way.

"No, I mean it – you are *so* good," she says, panting with the effort of keeping the leis spinning. "You must take after your mum and dad!"

I hadn't thought of it that way. My version of artistic-ness (and Rose Rouge's) is about a million miles from my parents'. But then I guess they had – once upon a time – been young and exciting art-school kids, before they got into snore-some stuff like reclaimed oak flooring and stainless steel worktops. . .

"Lemmie?"

I'm still smiling at Morven's sort-of compliment when she says my name.

"What?" I ask, as I try and wrestle the stepladder shut without trapping any useful fingers in it.

"Can I ask you something?"

"Er . . . sure," I say warily, wondering what's coming next.

"What exactly's the story with you and Sian Ellis?"

I'm not expecting that.

Morven seemed OK with my explanation yesterday outside the café (I'd said Sian was passing on some gossip about someone from our old school). Morven had seemed OK with my explanations the whole week, actually (even if I'm not sure about Jade).

I'm about to repeat all my cover stories again, when I realize I'm suddenly, *instantly* too tired to keep it all to myself.

"Are you all right, Lem?" Morven asks urgently, as I give up wrestling the stepladder shut and park my bum with a thud on the bottom rung instead. "Are you feeling ill again?"

"No . . . not really. It's just that I. . ."

It's just that I can't handle dragging round all these secrets any more. *Should* I tell her? Is this really safe? Can I maybe tell Morven *some* of the stuff without telling her *all* of the stuff? Can I just drop in bits about the friend-stealing and the bullying and miss out the psychologist and the "mad" jibes and everything?

"What's up, Lemmie? Can't you tell me?"

Bleep!

That's a text message.

My edited confessions about life with Sian the witch will have to wait a second; I need to see this in case it's important, i.e. in case it's from Rose Rouge.

"*R U ready?*"

OK, so that doesn't sound like Rose Rouge. Is it one of those spam texts? I wonder, scrolling down to read the rest.

"*Coz u r so gonna regret wot u said 2 me. . .*"

Sian.

It's from Sian.

My hands are shaking so much that I can hardly press the "delete" option on my mobile.

"What's it say, Lemmie? What's wrong?"

I've made a mistake; I nearly said too much. I wasn't safe at all.

"I – I better go, if everything's done," I tell Morven shakily. "See you later, just before four?"

"But, Lemmie. . .! *Lem!*"

As I run out of the barn towards home, all I can think of is, *how* did Sian Ellis get my mobile number. . .?

23

One last wild, wonderful weekend. . .

I've been lying very, very still on my bedroom floor for quite a long time now, just thinking.

Mum and Dad still aren't back from the show flats in Banchory, which means I can lie here without anyone coming to stare at me, like I've gone loopy or something.

Craig is staring at me – but with love, I like to think. I felt like a bit of company when I got back from doing up the barn, and so I pulled the hunk of quartz out of the skirting board in my room and laid a trail of biscuit crumbs from the knothole to my chest.

Sure enough, after ten minutes, Craig appeared.

And after another ten minutes or so of nervous nose-twitching and crumb-nibbling he eventually scampered up on to my chest, where he's now sitting, happily gnawing his way through a particularly big chunk of HobNob. He seems completely unbothered by the rise and fall of my breathing (hope he doesn't get motion-sickness).

Lying here, thinking, watching Craig, I'm starting to feel a lot calmer; a lot calmer than I was when I got Sian's text message at least. That's not to say I feel better . . . it's just that I've sort of accepted what's going to happen.

And what's going to happen is this: Sian Ellis is going to *properly* begin ruining my life here in Balgownie, starting as soon as she can, which will be Monday at school.

That's when she'll start spreading the stories. For instance, she'll tell anyone who'll listen about the time I freaked out Mrs O'Farrell by sneaking into the class early on her birthday, and hanging up all these streamers and decorations I'd made as a surprise. Dumb old me; I'd thought Mrs O'Farrell – and the rest of the class – would gasp at the prettiness of it all (and yes, the eleven-year-old me *was* kind of hoping it would make them like me more too). Instead, Mrs O'Farrell and everyone else acted horrified, as if I'd spray-painted swear-words round the classroom walls. It seemed like Mrs O'Farrell didn't appreciate anyone arty or eccentric or individual; she just liked good-as-gold girls like Sian. Sian, who helped her take down all the decorations, while I was in the headmistress's office, getting told how inappropriate my efforts had been and how bizarre my behaviour was.

Then they'll hear all the stuff about me running away from home, and being sent to the psychologist, and being a weirdo freak in general, and how everyone went out of their way to avoid me at our last school.

And once everyone hears this stuff, they'll take a look at my mismatching flip-flops, and remember the handstands, and the fooling around and the time I made my kneecaps dance to the theme tune of *EastEnders* and they'll think it's all nuts and not quirky any more.

And Morven and Jade? Well, they know more of my secrets than anyone else. They know about the marshmallow magic, and they know I nearly set the house on fire when I was writing Rose Rouge's name in the sky with my sparkler. They saw me do my wobbly-balancing act on the bridge last week, when they were begging me to come down.

What are they going to make of me after they hear what Sian's got to whisper and gossip about?

Like I've always worried, they probably won't want to stay friends.

But, hey – they're my friends for this one last day . . . and I'm going to enjoy every single second of it.

Listen to me! I feel like Cinderella, all of a sudden – up for a party even though I know that it's back to greyness and misery eventually. . .

Speaking about Jade's party, I better hurry and get ready soon, if that's the time already.

"Sorry to disturb you, Craig," I say, as I slowly start to sit up. "But I've got to go and get into my ballgown. . ."

"Wow . . . that dress is *pure* gorgeous, Lemmie!" sighs Jenna Harris, as I string a paper lei around her neck.

I've broken my own rules; despite the denim cut-offs, the flip-flops and the sunglasses propped on my head – holding back all the tiny plaits I braided my hair into – you can't exactly say that my outfit is totally tacky tourist. Originally, I'd planned to wear an old, ethnic-patterned short-sleeved shirt of Dad's, but as this was my last weekend of happiness, I decided I might as well go for it. . .

"You look great, Lem!" says Shonagh Roberts, reaching out and stroking the sleeve of the crimson velvet dress I'm wearing, borrowed from Rose Rouge.

I see Shonagh examining the dangling shell hearts

on the bracelet I'm wearing, but before she gets a chance to coo over that too, someone else speaks.

"What's this?" asks a voice I know pretty well.

Kyle Strachan is staring at the strings of leis that I've got hooked on my arm, ready to throw over every unsuspecting neck that arrives.

"They . . . they're called leis – it's a Hawaiian thing. To mean welcome." I grin nervously at him.

"What did she say that stuff was?" I hear Iain Whyte ask while I frantically rifle through the multi-coloured garlands to find the perfect lei for Kyle. With my hands shaking slightly, I grab a particularly gorgeous lime and raspberry one and go to hoist it over his head before he can complain.

"Oi, gerroff, you nutter!"

As Kyle ducks away laughing, my smile fades away and my arms stay fixed rigidly in mid-air, like a Sindy doll's. What he just said . . . it didn't sound funny, somehow. It sounded like a dig, like he might have really *meant* it, like someone might have got to him and told him –

"Can I have that pastel one? The one that's mostly pink?" says a syrupy-sweet, girlie voice.

My stiffened arms slowly lower as I clock Sian hovering directly behind a still-sniggering Kyle, Iain and Jack.

So . . . Sian has somehow invited herself along to

the party, using the lads for cover, after telling them *what*, exactly?

And then a certain truth dawns on me, like a roller blind whirling up to display the dazzling new day. Oh, yeah, same as 2+2=4, Sian Ellis got my mobile number one way and one way only.

Kyle.

Kyle Strachan.

How *could* he?

Well, that proves one thing . . . I was wrong; Sian *isn't* going to wait till Monday to destroy my life, she's started already and she's going to continue with her mission *right* here, *right* now. . .

"Shush! Everyone – that's Jade's mum on the phone with the code word!" shrieks Morven to the throngs of naffly dressed, lei-draped people already cramming the barn. "Jade's going to be here *any* second!"

But I won't.

Be here, I mean.

I can't handle Sian Ellis getting me back for standing up to her by spreading all my mad, bad, past history around the party.

I need to get out of here to somewhere I can breathe.

Now. . .

24

Walking in a summer winterland

Scotland likes to play tricks on you.

After weeks of biting cold winds and endless grey, drab days, it likes to surprise you, waking you up to gloriously bright, frost-speckled trees and such dazzling sunlight that you think you're on the set for some magical, fantasy film.

And then there's so-called summer, which means you could be basking in shimmering heatwaves or reaching for your jersey as the jagged-edged north wind hurtles in out of nowhere in particular – not even the north, like any sane person might expect.

Scotland is playing a trick on me now, as I sit on a boulder at the top of Craigandarroch hill, with the white-capped peaks of the Glentorran mountains off in the distance.

Oh, yes. The sun might be shining, but the breeze is suddenly blowing the lightest, dancing, unexpected flurry of snowflakes all around me. It's not the right time for flip-flops I guess. . .

Shivering, I clutch on to my knees and tilt my head back, opening my mouth wide to catch the tingling white flakes on my tongue.

I can't help myself; I start to giggle. Everything's too weird, too silly, too bizarre. But at least up here, it's also completely and stunningly beautiful, and I have it all to mysel—

"Wuff!"

I look around. For 360°, all I can see is billowing, pine-covered hills and mountains.

"Wuff!"

Closer to me, there's the cairn – the pile of stones you find at the top of lots of hills, that you're meant to add a stone to for luck – and as the hillside slips away, a jumble of scrubby bushes, ferns and weather-battered trees.

"Wuff!"

And then I see it: what looks like a red deer bounding through the greenery towards me.

Only it isn't so much bounding as galumphing, and deer don't tend to bark.

"Wuff!"

"Brick?" I say, as the dopey red setter thunders out of the undergrowth, with his tongue dangling happily out of his mouth.

Maybe Brick isn't as thick as people – including his owner Jade – think. Maybe deep down he's tuned into his genes as a tracker dog, sniffing out the trail my flip-flops left from the barn where Jade's grandparents had brought him for the party, to this spot, high above Balgownie.

"Lemmie?" a voice surprises me by calling out, just as Brick ignores my stroking hand and goes straight for my pockets, in case I've got anything interesting and edible in there. (Bad news for Brick; there's only half a packet of Lovehearts but he's giving that a go anyway.)

"Morven?" I frown, as my friend's fair-haired head appears down below, followed a second later by Jade's dark, shiny, bobbing hair.

"How. . .?"

I've lost my powers of speech, as my best friends struggle breathlessly towards me, in their good-for-parties/bad-for-hill-climbing outfits.

"How . . . did . . . we know . . . you were here?" Morven pants, collapsing down beside me.

"Kyle. . ." says Jade, kneeling down shivering in the moss at my feet. "He . . . he followed you."

"Why, to laugh at me and call me names some more?" I say bitterly.

"He . . . he *said* he thought you picked him up wrong," says Jade. "He didn't mean it, Lem. He said he was only fooling around and was gutted when you looked so hurt!"

"And then when you ran out," Morven takes over, rubbing her hands up and down her bare arms (a vest top isn't much good against jokey, freak Scottish snow flurries), "he followed you. He saw you running across the road and into the playpark, and then he said you disappeared."

"When he came back and told us," says Jade, zipping her thin, peppermint-green hooded top right up to the chin, "I said to Morv, 'Bet she'll be heading up Craigandarroch hill – on that other path that leads up from the playpark, since the path by the Lodge is sealed off!'"

So that's how well my friends know me – they know exactly where I'll come when I'm miserable. But that means I've ruined Jade's surprise. . .

"What about the party?" I say to her, feeling desperately sorry for messing up her birthday.

"It doesn't matter!" says Jade, her neat white teeth chattering. "What matters is *you*, Lemmie! Why did you run off? I saw you go when Mum and Dad drove up to the barn!"

"It wasn't just what Kyle said; it was something to do with Sian Ellis wasn't it?" Morven asks me, unwrapping a cardie from round her waist and quickly shoving her arms inside it.

"She didn't say anything to *me*," I murmur. "But I knew she was going to say *plenty*."

I drop my head down, and for a second, there's no sound apart from the wind whirling through the trees and the crunch of Lovehearts between doggy jaws.

"Kyle said she's been telling him stuff about you, about what happened at your old school," says Jade, kneeing her way closer to me till she's sidled up beside me and slipped her arm around my waist.

I appreciate her hug but my spirits slink to ground-level.

"Oh, God. . ." I mumble.

"Hey, don't panic!" says Morven, squishing up to me on the other side and wrapping her arm around my shoulders. "He said he can't stand Sian. He said she wangled her way into coming along to the party with him and Iain and Jack. He mentioned he had your mobile number, and she got it off him 'cause she said she wanted to ring you to see if it was all right, but he didn't really believe her. Then just after you left the party, he got really angry with her for calling you names just 'cause you had to go see a psychologist once."

Urgh . . . she's told everyone *everything* then.

"Three times, actually," I mutter, gloomily.

"Huh?"

"Three times. I went to see a child psychologist three times."

"One time . . . three times . . . whatever," says Jade. "The thing is, Sian chose the wrong person to bitch to about stuff like that – did you know Kyle's mum is a psychiatric nurse? Well, anyway, before he chased after you, Sian tried to make another bad taste joke about you and Kyle just totally flipped out at her, in front of everyone!"

A tiny glimmer of shininess and hope flickers inside of me, before the realization sinks in that Sian will have gone all out to justify herself to my classmates after that, pouring out *every* story she knows about me.

"Did she . . . did she say I ran away one time?"

"Yes. . ." says Morven, giving my shoulder a squeeze.

"And everyone thinks I'm crazy, right?" I whisper, raising my eyes enough to see the summer snowflakes swim in front of my eyes.

"Everyone thinks you're brilliant, Lemmie! They all just stared at Sian, till she realized that no one wanted to talk to her and she ran out!"

I'm tingling, and it's not just because I'm in the first stages of frostbite.

"They think I'm . . . what?"

"Lem – *everyone* at school thinks you're brilliant. You're like . . . like the mascot of our year!" says Jade.

"They don't think I'm mad. . .?"

"*Course* they do!" giggles Morven. "But that's why they like you, why me and Jade like you – you're the least dull person that's ever gone to Balgownie Academy!"

Close by us all, Brick is drooling sherbet-y froth, as he happily finishes crunching through my packet of Lovehearts, paper and plastic packaging and all. I feel so happy I could grab his frothy face and kiss it. If that didn't make me seem just that tiny bit *too* mad.

And then my heart suddenly goes *thunk*, like it's made from the heaviest boulder at the bottom level of the cairn.

Morven and Jade . . . they have to know. It's time I told them my deepest, darkest secret.

And after *this* bombshell, they might not be so keen to take my side.

"I've got to tell you. Something about Rose Rouge," I say, flipping my head from Morven's inquisitive face to Jade's impassive gaze.

"What about her?" says Morven.

What about her.

What about Rose Rouge.

What can I tell them about Rose Rouge, the one

person who's seen me through the worst times in the last few years, who's cheered me up when I've felt drowningly low, who's taught me to take on the world with a little sweet marshmallow magic?

Well, I can tell them this. . .

"Rose Rouge. . ." I say, not sure if I can get the words out.

Jade and Morven stare at me, as the snowflakes flutter into nothingness and the sun begins to beam down on our shoulders to warm our souls.

"She. . ."

I can do this.

I've *got* to do this.

"Rose Rouge doesn't exist."

There – I've said it. . .

25

Truths, half-truths and where-are-you? texts

Jade's surprise party is going great.

Apparently.

The food – Scottish, Chinese *and* Hawaiian – is a success, everyone's dancing (still wearing their shades), Danny Wilson's doing kung-fu moves on the balloons floating about and everyone's having a brilliant time.

Course, they *are* wondering when the birthday girl will be back so they can cut the birthday cake – which has tartan ribbon and icing-sugar lotus flowers on it, Shonagh Roberts says.

But Jade insists she's not in any rush. She wants to know everything and understand everything, however long that takes. Even if the waitresses of the Balgownie café are giving us dark glowers for taking up a table which they'd really like to be clearing so they can lock up for the day.

(Tied up outside, Brick is giving us an impatient glower of his own.)

"So she was your make-believe, childhood friend, then?"

I nod at Morven, and clasp my hands tighter around my milkshake.

I've just explained it all to them. All about Rose Rouge, how she started life when I was small and was jealous of my friends in Edinburgh who had sisters and brothers and dogs and cats to play with, when all I had were nice but permanently busy parents.

So to keep me company I invented Rose, my imaginary playmate, my imaginary sister, even. The name is mine; I'm Laurel Rosalie Ferguson, and at six years old, I felt too small to need all those names for myself.

"Back then, I used to think she looked like Isla," I grin, thinking of my scruffy door angel. "And my parents thought it was cute – they even used to set a place at the table for her!"

"And then?" asks Jade, in her usual, straight-to-the-point way.

"And then I grew out of her, totally forgot about Rose. Till Sian started at my primary school, when

I was about nine. Once the bullying started and every-one began to chum up to Sian, I needed someone to be on my side. So Rose Rouge came back. And my parents weren't so keen this time round. . ."

I guess it's one thing to have an imaginary friend when you're a dimple-cheeked little kid, but there's something too weird about it as you get older, specially since I started giving her more of a character. I landed her with the nickname of Rose Rouge after I saw it under a paint swatch in one of Mum and Dad's decorating brochures, and gave myself a nickname too, while I was at it. I decided Rose Rouge now looked like a dreadlocked hippy girl I saw on TV at the Glastonbury festival, crossed with photos of my mum from when she was younger. It all made a weird kind of comforting sense to me at the time.

But suddenly Mum and Dad kind of froze when I mentioned her, not understanding quite *why* I needed a friend. And they were too busy with making a life and a living for all of us, I s'pose, to listen to me properly.

"I did do lots of stuff that completely freaked them out, like painting my whole room red one day after I found this antique blusher pot called 'Rose Rouge' in a car boot sale and getting all inspired."

"Wait!" says Morven, slapping her hands so hard on the table that all the cutlery vibrates. "I remember you telling me about this! You said it was one of the wild things Rose Rouge did!"

I smile ruefully. Every one of the wild things Rose Rouge did was something that actually happened to *me*, but the true-life story was never as much fun as the version I spun for Rose. Like the day I tried to dress up for school, or decorate my classroom, or when I found that sad, stray dog snuffling round the bins outside our flats and tried to hide it in my room, so it could be my secret pet. (Mum and Dad took it to the SSPCA when they found it, its muzzle covered in cream from the doughnuts I'd fed it.) I'd even made Rose Rouge's version of the running-away story sound like an adventure, when all it had been was scary and lonely, sitting on that old, grumbly bus to Perth, not knowing where it was I'd arrived at.

"But you always said she came to Balgownie to visit you!" Jade frowns at me.

Wow. It feels amazing and scary to get all these secrets off my chest.

"I guess. . ." I continue hesitantly, "I guess this last year in Balgownie, I've been really happy, but Rose Rouge, she'd just got to be a habit. I didn't need her so much – 'cause I had you two to hang out with – so I just sort of invented this life she had at art school, where she was busy all the time and stuff. It's just that I liked to know I could imagine her coming to visit, now and then, like an old friend. . ."

I taper off, sure I sound completely barking.

"What about all the stuff you said she gave you? Like that blue plastic garland that made you come up with the idea for the party decorations?" Morven asks, trying to understand. "Or that velvet dress you've got on?"

Ah, all the silly, kitsch presents that Rose Rouge bought me from a corny Pound store. Or, putting it another way, all the silly, kitsch presents I bought *myself* from the Pound store whenever Mum took me through to Aberdeen shopping. And the dress? I got it in a sale in TopShop, same as the cherries T-shirt. . .

"Lemmie, what about the marshmallow magic?" says Jade. "You always said Rose Rouge taught you that!"

The marshmallow magic. . . The marshmallow magic that cushioned and protected me through all the bad times with Sian. The marshmallow magic that I'd got so used to trusting in that I'd never known how I could handle the days or the weeks without its power working in the background, propping up my world around the edges.

"I made it up," I admit, feeling suddenly smaller than Craig the mini-mouse.

"Yeah, so you made it all up," Jade agrees, sounding brutally harsh for a second. "But underneath, it was just stuff to give you confidence. People write features about that sort of thing all the time in magazines, so don't feel bad about it!"

"That's right!" Morven joins in. "It's like those programmes on telly, where they talk about how to feel better about yourself, if you feel shy or whatever!"

"Anyway, Rose Rouge was just like a superhero version of you, really, wasn't she, Lem?" says Jade suddenly.

I glance down into my strawberry milkshake as Jade speaks, and all I can think of is the fact that:

a) I have the best, most understanding friends a girl could hope for,

b) that's why I'd started to imagine Rose Rouge coming to me less and less often (I didn't need her), and

c) I might cry.

"Hey – I just remembered. What about that photo you showed us?" Morven suddenly asks me. "The one in the snow dome? The one that was supposed to be Rose Rouge?"

"That was my mum, when she was sixteen, just before she went to art school," I tell her. "Around the time she met my dad."

Hence the family resemblance.

Oh, God, it's such a jumbled mess.

Can I really expect Morven and Jade to totally understand my whole tangled gloop of secrets and lies?

Bleep!

"It's from Shonagh," mutters Jade, looking at the text on her mobile screen and checking her latest party update from our classmate. "She says '*Where R U 3? Get back here partying NOW!*'"

"What are we waiting for?" grins Morven.

"Yeah, come on!" laughs Jade. "The biggest surprise of my surprise party is that I've not properly turned up at it yet!"

For the first time ever, Jade's made a half-decent joke.

Which is why I'm laughing, maybe a bit too hard.

But I can't remember ever feeling this happy.

"By the way," says Jade, as we all get up from the table. "Me and Morv – we never really believed Rose Rouge existed."

I'm nearly too shocked to say anything, but I manage to squeak out a "How come?"

"'Cause we never met her," Morven says her piece. "'Cause you never mentioned her in front of anyone else at school. 'Cause I only saw *you* on your own that time I was walking in the woods with my dad and brother – and you were wearing *that* velvet dress."

"But we didn't care," Jade adds, fixing her dark eyes on me and smiling, "'cause we liked *you*, Lemmie. And anyway, it all makes more sense now. When Sian was being a real witch to you, it was like you had to invent your own white witch to protect yourself, didn't you?"

Once upon a time, I said that when it came to my secrets, Rose Rouge knew everything about everything. Well, that's not a *total* lie, since Rose Rouge is part of *me*, and I guess I should know all my own secrets better than anyone.

The only secret I had but didn't see was that I have the best two friends in the whole (real) world. . .

26

Minus the marshmallow magic. . .

"It looks awesome!"

"Shut up, Kyle," I say, grinning as much as I'm blushing.

"Go on, stand there, so I can take a picture!" he orders, lifting up his digital camera and pointing me to stand in front of one the hoardings circling Craigandarroch woods.

"No! Don't take my photo!" I protest, overcome with shyness and hiding my face in my hands. "Tell him, Jade!"

But Jade's too busy gawping to pay any attention to my general feebleness.

"Lemmie, are you crazy? *You* did all this – check it

out!" insists Kyle. "Check out the whole thing!"

I can't. It's too much – like how I imagine it would be to look at the unimaginable, breathtaking vastness of the Grand Canyon and then come out with something naff and useless like, "Yeah, it's quite nice!"

Not that I'm comparing some stupid little artworks of mine to the Grand Canyon (urgh, how vain do *I* sound?).

I just mean that when you've done some small collages of your town and had them photographed and blown up to *gigantic* proportions and stuck on to loads of advertising hoardings, it's pretty hard to look at them all without blushing, *that's* all I'm saying.

"Look – there's the original one!" I hear Morven calling out and glance up in time to see her hurrying over to a humungous version of the collage I made of the Lodge, lemon slice window and all.

Sian's dad – he saw my collage at the parents' night at school and decided my style – with all the natural elements – was perfect for the image the new spa resort was trying to represent. He wanted to commission me to do more, to plaster them on the white boards that blocked the view of what was going on in Craigandarroch woods.

I took some convincing, of course. Ms McIver said it was what every artist dreamed of: getting exhibited *and* getting paid. But I still couldn't bring myself to say yes, not when I resented the fact that the Lodge and the woods were being crushed out of existence by a bulldozer or three. Then Mum and Dad got involved, and told me Mr Ellis had invited us all for a sight inspection (non-flattering hard-hats included) to see what exactly was going on behind the screened-off fencing at Craigandarroch. . .

I guess it was when I found out that not a branch of the woods was going to be touched ("It's a health spa, Laurel! Nature trails are absolutely fundamental to what we believe in!") that I started to wobble. Then, when I stood with Mum and Dad in front of the old Lodge – the three of us in our ridiculous matching hard-hats – I melted.

Yeah, so they were knocking down most of the Lodge – at least, the parts that were so rotted and crumbly they were beyond saving – but they were keeping the frontage, with the curlicues and turrets, and the grand front door and lemon-slice circular window. They'd already cut back the waist-high grass of the lawn and started to follow age-old plans of planting, just how it would have been back when the Lodge was first built.

"Maybe you'll miss the dragonflies," Mr Ellis had smiled at me, "but when the original rose gardens are back in place, it'll be a paradise for butterflies!"

Poor Mr Ellis . . . he was so nice I couldn't say no to taking his very large cheque for doing the advertising posters after that. And I felt sorry for him too – people can't help having the children they have. And I don't know; maybe he was quite pleased – like me and everyone at school – when his wife and daughter decided after only a couple of weeks in Balgownie to go back to Edinburgh and let him live on his own up here for the year.

It's a shame Sian felt like she didn't fit in, isn't it?

(Answer: you've *got* to be joking. . .)

"Hey, I bet you'll be able to see all the way over here out of your new bedroom windows!" says Morven, spinning her head around so fast that I see a sparkle of silver from the chain of her Luckenbooth. (I bought Jade one, too, from the same shop in Aberdeen I originally bought mine. It's like our sisterhood symbol.)

"Yeah – when are the builders going to be finished, Lem?" asks Jade, as she bends over and starts gathering a handful of buttercups growing by the edge of the metal fencing.

"Next week, I think."

Mum and Dad – normally they're flapping over other people's projects, but now they're flapping over my room, narking at the builders to hurry up since they promised me the work wouldn't take too long, and I'd be back in my beloved (but extended) attic by the end of the holidays.

But I don't mind too much. The view I'm going to get out of the huge windows – right the way over to the Glentorran mountains, to the Tor-na-Dee ski-slopes, to Craigandarroch itself – is going to be (as Kyle would say) awesome. And the spare room downstairs is OK to sleep in too – it isn't so cold and clinical now I've strung up my chilli-pepper lights and Blu-tacked my paper butterflies on the walls.

It helps that I've got company, too. Craig seems quite happy now he's an official pet, in his official five-star cage with luxury sleeping quarters (my hand-painted bamboo box, lined with feathers), never mind the endless food supplies. Mum doesn't love it when I let him out – she thinks he'll escape back behind the skirting boards and start a colony of mice. But I know, when I watch him scampering up my arm for the piece of apple I'm tempting him with, he's too chubby (in his own tiny way) to squeeze through knotholes any more.

Things are better with Mum and Dad, if you hadn't noticed. The night of Jade's party, Jade and Morven came to mine to sleep over. The two of them bullied me – in the nicest, kindest way – into telling Mum and Dad *everything*, with them sitting on either side of me for support, filling in the gaps when thoughts of Sian turned my tongue into a knot.

That's when I knew for sure that real live friends were better than imaginary sisters. It was also when me and my parents realized other stuff, like *they* needed lessons in listening properly, and *I* needed lessons in not bottling things up. My parents and me, we all promised to try lots, lots harder, which is why I let them persuade me that doing up my room would be cool, and *they* let themselves be persuaded that pets – especially minuscule ones – were actually kind of nice. (I haven't told them that Brick's just fathered a litter of very cute red setter puppies . . . yet.)

Suddenly, a flutter of wings makes me blink. It's a butterfly – a red admiral. Maybe it's checking out my artworks on the hoardings too, or maybe it's just hovering around, impatient for the promised rose gardens.

"Hey, don't move!" says Kyle. "It's landed right on your head!"

I don't dare to breathe, as Kyle lifts the camera and snaps me with my living, breathing, quivering hair ornament. But I'm also finding it hard to breathe because there are times – like this – when me and Kyle look into each other's eyes, even via a camera lens, and it makes us both blush and fumble. Yeah, so we hang out together all the time now, ever since Jade's party, and I love having him as a friend. But what'll happen next? Well, one thing's for sure . . . I'm not looking for any mystical signs for clues. I've kind of given up on marshmallow magic.

Yep, it's true. Me, Jade and Morven had a little ritual farewell to lots of the marshmallow magic down by the bridge a few weeks ago, letting my shoebox-worth of feathers flutter downstream, dropping stuff like my dice and my rose quartz into the water with a satisfying splosh.

"Hey, Lemmie – how much did you say you got paid for doing these pictures?" asks Jade, straightening up now she's finished gathering her mini-bouquet.

"Quite a lot," I say. "Why?"

"Enough to treat us all to an ice cream at the café?" she grins.

"Yeah, I guess so! C'mon!"

As me, Morven, Jade and Kyle leave Craigandarroch behind and head off along the dusty road towards town, something catches my eye.

"Oh, hold on. . ."

Out of habit, I bend down and pick up a feather – a starling's – which would have taken my collection (including the bundle in Craig's bed) up to 374.

OK, so life's changed for me here in Balgownie,

and I've kind of given up on secrets, and marshmallow magic and Rose Rouge.

But do you want to know a secret? I don't think I can *totally* give up on seeing things as marshmallow-flavoured or rose-tinted.

If you don't believe me, just ask Isla, my Bag Angel, who's pinned inside my rucksack right now, looking out for my Hello Kitty purse and my hairbrush and my lucky fossil and that half-finished packet of Munchies. . .

About the Author

In her teens, Karen McCombie vowed three things: one, to be an artist; two, never to move away from Scotland; and three, never to get married. Strangely enough, she is now a full-time author living in leafy north London with her husband, Tom.

The lure of work on magazines such as *J17* and *Sugar* was the reason for the move south, and after several years in journalism, Karen turned her attention to fiction, writing the best-selling series Ally's World, as well as Stella Etc. and many more teen titles.

In her spare time, Karen likes to stop and pat cats in the street, even though she has three at home.

There's always something going on in ALLY'S WORLD

the PAST, the PRESENT and the LOUD, LOUD GIRL

My family's weird. I know everyone says that, but we are definitely weird. My eldest sister is **17** going on **70**, my other sister is away with the fairies (literally – her room is a shrine to whoever invented fairy lights) and my little brother is a space cadet who's obsessed with Rolf Harris. Me? Somehow I ended up normal, but it's a struggle, let me tell you ... and I will tell you – soon as I get this vibrating three-legged cat off my head...

DATES, DOUBLE DATES and BIG, BIG TROUBLE

OK, so my dad's started ironing his jeans (yes, really) – something must be up. I mean, why would he slick back his hair to meet the plumber? It can only mean one thing – Dad is Seeing Someone. Like, a Woman Someone. And it can't be our mum, because she's still off travelling the world. There's only one thing for it – serious sisterly espionage. Hey, I know it's sneaky, but we have to uncover the awful (cringeworthy) truth...

3 BUTTERFLIES, BULLIES and Bad, Bad Habits

Rowan's been acting strange (well, OK, more strange than usual). One minute she's crying over who-knows-what, and the next she's tripping into the house with all this new stuff (which has to come from the shopping fairy, since I know she's got zero money). Then there's the graffiti at school: "Rowan Love is a muppet" (and I don't think it's meant in a friendly, Kermit-is-cool kind of way). Just what is going on with my sister?

4 FRIENDS, FREAK-OUTS and VERY SECRET SECRETS

OK, so I did have a best friend called Sandie, but I think she's been replaced by a Star-Trek type android. She still looks like Sandie, but since when did my real friend copy everything I do, and storm off in big huffs over nothing? I think the same thing's happened to Kyra's mum – the super-witch mum from hell Kyra's always moaning about actually seems super-nice. Have all my mates gone mad, or have I stumbled into Crouch End in a parallel universe...?!

BOYS, bROTHERS and JELLY-BELLY dancing

Boys are weird things ... and just lately, the boys in my life have been acting even more weird. Take Billy, for example. He's been behaving like a total muppet (as the whole bra-on-head incident proves), and what's worse is I've been having unexplained feelings (like – eek! – lovey, jealous type feelings) for the big dweeb (scary). Not only that, but Tor's been acting strange too – something to do with boy mice, girl mice, and Mum. Confused? You're not the only one...

SISTERS, SUPER-CREEPS and SLUSHY, GUSHY LOVE SONGS

So Linn isn't usually the most approachable elder sister (about as approachable as a grumpy wasp), but her "My family drives me mad!!" face has definitely been appearing more often lately. Maybe trespassing in her sacred room to answer her mobile wasn't one of my best ideas... Still, now we know that Linn's got a boyfriend – Q, lead singer in Chazza's band. Linn thinks he's super-cool, so why do me and Rowan get the distinct impression that he's actually a super-creep...?

PARTIES, PREDICAMENTS and UNDERCOVER PETS

So there I was, thinking that the last week of school was going to be mega-fun – I mean, there's the *Fun Run*, the end of term party ... **OK**, well more fun than usual. Could I have been more wrong? Urm, no. I mean, next-door's barbecue degenerates into a sausage fight, I nearly have to call the RSPCA on Kyra, the *Fun Run* is more of a No-fun Limp and, oh yes, how could I forget that disastrous game of Spin the Bottle...

8

TATTOOS, TELLTALES and TERRIBLE, TERRIBLE TWINS

Hurray! Summer holidays – nothing to do but laze around, hang out with my mates and have fun. Then Dad announces that his long-lost brother is coming to stay – cue Ricki Lake-style tearful reunion and every-one living happily ever after... Hmm, maybe not. Turns out that Uncle Joe comes complete with witchy wife and evil, pet-torturing twins. And evil girl twin seems determined to annoy all my friends, scare off my not-quite-boyfriend and generally ruin my life. *Fun*? If this is fun, I'm Kylie Minogue...

MATES, MYSTERIES PRETTY WEIRD WEIRDNESS

Spooky stuff's been happening lately. I mean, one little love spell and next thing I know me and my mates are running round Queen's Woods scared stupid. Then there are the mysteriously disappearing garden gnomes that have been reappearing in very odd places, and the weird noises and strangely misplaced knick-knacks (er, OK, that's not that odd in our disaster-zone of a house...). But here's the strangest thing: what exactly is going on between Billy and one of my best girl friends...?

DAISY, DAD and the HUGE, SMALL SURPRISE

Love is in the air! Billy and Sandie are getting a bit sick-makingly gooey, Grandma and Stanley are getting hitched, and Dad and Tor's new teacher are getting along just a little too well... As for me, Rowan and Linn, we're just getting scared – Grandma's told us our bridesmaid get-up has to be pastel-coloured. Pastel? Blee! But a looming fashion disaster isn't the main thing that's bothering me – I can't help feeling someone important's been forgotten in all this love stuff. Er, Mum, for example?

11 RAINBOWS, ROWAN and TRUE, TRUE ROMANCE(?)

Alfie, Alfie, Alfie ... how deeply cool can one boy be? And not only is he drop-dead yum, but he's sweet and kind and has single-handedly turned Rowan into a local celeb! So why is Linn less than chuffed about this? And, um, why do I find myself taking the Grouch Queen's side for once? Well, my sisters might be having hissy fits at each other, but at least Mum and Dad are definitely back together, right? Er, wrong...

12 VISITORS, VANISHINGS and VA-VA-VA VOOM

Well, zut alors ... as if by magic, a whole bunch of very cute French boys has just turned up in Crouch End. (OK, so it's not by magic, it's 'cause of a school exchange trip. Oh, and there're girls too.) Me and most of mes amies are desperate to get close enough to torture them with our terrible French. All mes amies except Jen, that is – who's just pulled a vanishing act. Uh-oh...

3

CRUSHES, CLIQUES and the COOL, SCHOOL TRIP

Yeah! Me and my mates are skiving school for a whole week! (Kind of...) We're all prepared for our geography field trip (apart from Kyra, who's dressed like she's going for a hike around TopShop). Only downer is, before we even get on the coach Sandie's pining miserably for Billy. But who'd have thought she'd recover so quickly...? Must be those super new friends she's made for us – er, make that super new enemies...

4

HASSLES, HEART-PINGS! and Sad, HAPPY ENDINGS...

Well, knock me down with a feather – just not one with superglue on (don't ask). The weirdness going on in my world means my head's even twistier than normal. First Sandie's parents break some big news, then Linn makes a scary announcement, and to top it all there's the, er, heated incident with Rowan and her Johnny Depp shrine. Nothing else could possibly surprise me ... not even if I opened the front door and found that I had a boyfriend on the doorstep... (Fat chance!)

for more gossip check out
www.karenmccombie.com

WELCOME TO A WHOLE NEW WORLD...

☆ STELLA ETC. ☆

The sunshiney, seasidey, gorgeous new series from Karen McCombie

① FRANKIE, PEACHES & ME

Stella can't believe her luck. Seb – the boy she's liked for for ever – told her he liked her too. At her leaving party. (Talk about bad timing...) Yep, as of today, her family's swapped life in London for a sleepy seaside resort where the biggest thrill is a psycho seagull. But how is shy-girl Stella going to fit into this freaky little town, especially without her best friend Frankie? And what's with the suspicious silence from all her other mates back in London? Then – in a waft of peaches and cream – a mysterious furry someone wanders into Stella's life, and things instantly start to get interesting...

2 SWEET-TALKING TJ

Stella's getting used to her new life in the sleepy seaside town of Portbay, but it's still a no-friend-zone (unless you count friends of the weird, furry, catty kind). So when she spots a scruffy, cute, friendly-looking boy on the beach Stella hopes he might be a potential new mate – him *and* his barking mad dog, Bob. But it seems TJ already has some dodgy mates of his own… Stella's confused. Why is sweet, goofball TJ hanging round with a bunch of total meatheads…?

3 MEET THE REAL WORLD, RACHEL

Stella's got a new best mate (the small but cute TJ), and things in Portbay are now much more fun (like the hoax they're planning with the camera and the, er, fairies). The only hassle is Rachel and her gang, who still manage to make Stella feel like she doesn't fit in… But then all this weird stuff happens to Rachel, and her so-called friends start avoiding her. Has she been taken over by aliens, like TJ thinks? (Duh…) And should Stella come to Rachel's rescue, or is that possibly the worst idea she's ever had…?

Out now:

4 TRULY, MADLY MEGAN